SEED SAVERS

LILY

What Readers Are Saying About *Seed Savers: Lily*

"A creative, engaging, well-written series filled with action and a lot of truth as it touches the very real issue of preserving seeds from Greedy Corporate Seed Monopoly and understanding the importance of knowing how to grow our own healthy food. This book series is AWESOME!!!!!!!"

—RACHEL PARENT, Teen Founder of Kids Right to Know

"In *Lily*, the second book of the *Seed Savers* series, young people continue to secretly grow vegetables, an illegal act in their world. They form diverse friendships across ethnic lines as they search for truth behind unanswered questions. *Lily* encourages readers to bravely work for a better world."

—JOYCE YODER, former educator, Salem-Keizer Schools

"My tween son LOVED the first two *Seed Savers* books . . . *Lily* is the story of the child left behind with the gardening contraband while her friends went on the run. It takes place at the same time as the second half of book one, *Treasure*. The setting and problem have already been established, so book two flowed easily right from the very first page. The language read smoothly, naturally, with beautiful word pictures and a very nice pace. Overall, I thought the artistry was remarkable. I'm eager to read book three!"

—MICHELLE ISENHOFF, tween author and blogger

"With the arrival of *Lily*, I expected to get 'the further adventures of Clare and Dante,' but what I got was much more. Lily, a side character in the first book, *Treasure*, continues the mission of saving seeds in her hometown after the disappearance of Clare and Dante. Rather than getting *Treasure* all over again, a common fault in sequels in general, *Lily* is a book all its own and full of secrets, secrets, and more secrets. Smith succeeds again in writing a fantastic and educational adventure . . . It is fun and refreshing to read something new, something real, that doesn't have anything to do with vampires, werewolves, or zombies. *Seed Savers* is about using your brain, questioning the world around you, becoming a better person, and making the world a better place. These are things every kid should be encouraged to do. And for adults reading these books it reminds us that kids want to, when given the chance."

—ANDI KLEMM, *Anakalian Whims*

"*Lily* is a delightful read that continues the *Seed Savers* series. I love how the futuristic world is grounded in reality. The character development keeps progressing over each book. Smith has created an intriguing read that has me on the edge of my seat for each book."

—KANDI J. WYATT, tween author and blogger

"Lily is not just a secondary character in the *Seed Savers* series. She is interesting, complex, and extremely likable. Getting to know Lily and her story was a pleasant surprise. I found that I liked Lily a lot and want to know what she does next. I'm rooting for her to find what she is looking for! I'm surprised I liked the second book in the series even more than the first. I'm looking forward to reading book three to see where Smith takes us next."

—RITA NELSON, middle school teacher/librarian

"*Lily* is a well-written dystopian book with a great story."

—ERIK WEIBEL, *This Kid Reviews Books*

"This series fills the void for younger-audience dystopians. Even so, older readers will love it too!"

—*My Full Bookshelf Reviews*

"I have read *Seed Savers* books one and two and can hardly wait for the third one. As an avid gardener and teacher, this series offers much to both aspects . . . The characters are engaging and believable in their adventures. I highly recommend this series to anyone who would like to awaken in our children to be the change they want to see."

—SALLY WHITE, former science and gardening teacher, Green Apple Award Winner, and Straub Environmental Learning Center All-Star Volunteer

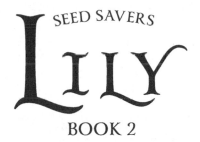

SEED SAVERS

LILY

BOOK 2

SANDRA SMITH

**FLYING
BOOKS
HOUSE**

SALEM, OREGON

Flying Books House
2514 Hazel Avenue Northeast
Salem, Oregon 97301

FlyingBooksHouse.com
SeedSaversSeries.com

This is a work of fiction. Names, characters, businesses, places, events and incidents are either the products of the author's imagination or used in a fictitious manner. Any resemblance to actual persons, living or dead, or actual events is purely coincidental.

ISBN 978-1-943345-09-0 paperback
ISBN 978-1-943345-08-3 ebook
ISBN 978-1-943345-10-6 hardcover

Book Design by Shannon Bodie, BookWise Design
Cover Art by Alan Baker

An earlier edition of this book was first published by Sandra L. Smith in 2012.

Publisher's Cataloging-In-Publication Data
(Prepared by The Donohue Group, Inc.)

Names: Smith, Sandra (Sandra Louise), 1962-
Title: Seed savers. Book 2, Lily / Sandra Smith.
Other Titles: Lily
Description: Salem, Oregon : Flying Books House, [2018] | Originally published: [Oregon] : Sandra Smith, 2012. | Includes bibliographical references and list of resources for further reading. | Interest age level: 10 and up. | Summary: "In a future where gardening is illegal, and corporations decide what people eat, thirteen-year-old Lily defies the status quo by planting the banned seeds entrusted to her by friends--friends who have disappeared under mysterious circumstances. She sets out to discover more about the secret organization with which they were involved. Her investigation unearths a disturbing secret from her own past, unsettling her world even more."-- Provided by publisher.
Identifiers: ISBN 9781943345090 (paperback) | ISBN 9781943345106 (hardcover) | ISBN 9781943345083 (ebook)
Subjects: LCSH: Seeds--Juvenile fiction. | Vegetable gardening--Juvenile fiction. | Corporate power--Juvenile fiction. | Future life--Juvenile fiction. | CYAC: Seeds-- Fiction. | Vegetable gardening--Fiction. | Corporate power--Fiction. | Future life-- Fiction. | LCGFT: Dystopian fiction.
Classification: LCC PZ7.1.S6557 Sel 2018 (print) | LCC PZ7.1.S6557 (ebook) | DDC [Fic]--dc23

Printed in the United States of America

For Louise and Percy Schmeiser.

CONTENTS

*When I let go of what I am,
I become what I might be.*

LAO TZU

1

MISSING!

My name is Lily. When I first heard Clare and Dante were missing and presumed runaway, I couldn't believe it. Clare is my best friend, after all, and her brother Dante like the brother I never had. Hadn't I just seen them? Didn't I see them practically every day of my life? They weren't the kind of kids who run away.

When I learned the rest of the story, the pieces started falling into place. Clare's mom had been arrested on charges of illegal plant possession. It was only one plant—a tomato—but it was highly illegal. And I knew something the cops didn't know: I knew the tomato plant belonged to Clare, Dante, and me. I knew we were the ones involved in the unlawful activities of saving seeds and growing food. I knew our friend Ana, the senior citizen who was our mentor, had recently disappeared.

A simple runaway case? Definitely not. Clare and Dante ran to save their mother. They ran to save the seeds. They ran to save the future and the present, and something of the past.

It was my mom who first told me about Clare and Dante's disappearance. Actually, it was more like an interrogation, only gentler, because it was Ma. She asked me all sorts of questions starting with *when did you last see either of them* and ending with *no one has seen the siblings in twenty-four hours.* Apparently the cops visited our place because Clare and I are friends. The homes of all friends and classmates were checked.

That's the story the police gave Ma anyway. As I would find out later, those same cops had jailed Mrs. James earlier in the day. All Ma knew was that my best friends in the whole world were missing and she wanted to make sure I wasn't harboring important information. The police assured Ma it looked like a runaway case rather than an abduction—their bikes and backpacks were gone—so at least she wasn't freaking out that I might get kidnapped.

The fact was, I hadn't seen Clare and Dante since Sunday. It was summer break so there wasn't the daily interaction of school. Besides that, they were attending tech day camp. I was not.

After Ma questioned me, I tried to remember my last conversation with Clare. Were my friends having family troubles that would cause them to leave? I couldn't believe they would act so drastically. I would know if something was up, wouldn't I? My only conclusion was that Clare and Dante were forced to leave, or left in a hurry—unable to tell me.

As soon as I got the chance I rode my bike to Clare and Dante's apartment. Yellow police tape surrounded the cement stoop where we had often sat talking and conspiring. The door to the flat hung open. Empty. I wondered where their mother was.

Something's not right. I rode out of sight and watched from across the street behind a parked truck. That's when I saw *him* with the local police, a man from GRIM, the Green Resource Investigation Machine. A federal enforcer of all things plant and food related.

I sped home and raced to my room, closing and locking the door behind me. I was out of breath, but not from the physical exertion. In one of my last conversations with Clare she had shared her fears that something had happened to Ana. Ana had missed church—the only place the two of them felt safe meeting—and it worried Clare. I told her to calm down, that she was overreacting.

And now Clare and Dante were gone too.

After mulling over the situation and considering options of what to do, I decided to keep a low profile.

Maybe Clare and Dante were hiding somewhere for a reason I had yet to discover.

Either way, I didn't like the way people were disappearing. I stayed home the next day. Ma appreciated the extra help folding the tiny paper cranes she sold for income in gift stores and craft bazaars.

On Friday I rode to Clare's place again. The yellow tape was gone, and a light was on inside. I rode up and propped my bicycle against the building. I couldn't help gazing toward the place our carrots had fiercely grown like the outlaws they were. Gone! The ground torn up with no trace of the carrots we'd lovingly and patiently tended. I sidled up the stairs and knocked.

The door opened. Clare's mom, more harried and haggard-looking than ever, stood waiting. Dark circles hung under her eyes like rain clouds in the late autumn sky. I could tell she hadn't slept and had probably been crying.

"Lily!"

She lunged to hug me. I don't know what came over me. I was relieved to find her, of course, but beyond my will and to my embarrassment, tears welled up and spilled down my face. We held each other crying in the doorway for several minutes. Then Celia let go and ushered me in, urging me to sit.

That's when I learned about her arrest for the tomato plant.

"I spoke to Clare on the phone from jail," Celia said. "But they held me two more days. When I called the second day, no one answered. Those damned cops wouldn't let me call again. They told me not to worry. I knew somethin' was wrong."

I listened quietly.

"Lily, where are my kids?"

I was torn on how to respond. I knew more than Celia did, but Clare always felt the less her mother knew the better off she would be.

"I don't know," I answered truthfully. "The police think they left on their own." The words "ran away" seemed too harsh to say aloud.

"Yes," Celia admitted. "Both backpacks, bikes, a flashlight, food—all gone. It don't look like no kidnappin'."

We sat, silent. At last I said, "They're together. Clare will take care of Dante."

Celia clasped my hand and smiled a little, her cheeks glistening with tears.

"Thanks for that," she whispered. "But why? Why did they go?" Her dark and hollowed eyes bored into me.

I shrugged my shoulders. I had a pretty good idea it had something to do with GRIM and the seized plant, but my head was still spinning with my own selfish question: *Why didn't they take me?*

2

SEARCHING FOR ANSWERS

So there I was, midsummer and suddenly my best friends had disappeared. The only thing that kept me going was tending the vegetables I'd planted around town.

You can say I'm a bad friend if you want. Clare had entrusted me with the bulk of Ana's seeds and I'd gone ahead and sown some this season. Clare hadn't agreed when I suggested planting in vacant lots around town; she wanted to start slowly, preparing and planning first, waiting until next year. But I couldn't wait. I had sneaked out and planted anyway. And my seeds had prospered. I had fine-looking plants hidden all over the neighborhood. I had planned to tell Clare sooner or later, I really had.

Visiting my plants now was good therapy as I tried to figure out why Clare and Dante ran, why they didn't tell me, and where they might be headed. But as inspirational as the crunchy red radishes were, I couldn't discover any answers. From what I knew of my friend I guessed Clare ran away to protect her mom, and she *didn't* run here to protect me. Or maybe she thought GRIM would stop us so she ran to continue the Movement . . . Where she ran to, I didn't have a clue.

The more I thought about it, the best answer was that maybe she and Dante tried to find Ana. We both had maps to Ana's house. But what if that wasn't it? What if Ana, Clare, and Dante *had* been captured by GRIM, and GRIM only made it look like Clare and Dante ran away? Would I be next to disappear? A chill ran down my spine as I imagined my mom sitting at the kitchen table folding origami alone.

I couldn't stand it any longer. In my daily rides around town checking my secret gardens, I saw no evidence of GRIM agents—I had to try to find Ana's house.

That evening, after sufficient small talk with Ma, I excused myself to my room. Digging out the map Ana had given us in case of emergency, I carefully studied the route to her house. It might take half an hour by bike. I hatched a plan.

The next morning I arose early, leaving a note on the table for Ma. I apologized for not asking permission and told her I'd be out all day with the family of a friend—told her I was lonely without Clare. Part of it was true. I assured her the whole family would be along since Ma was careful like that. I even threw in a name to make it seem real: *my friend, Rose,* I wrote. I loaded my backpack with emergency supplies and stuffed my pockets with loose change. After applying sunscreen carefully, I fastened on a microhelmet topped with a wide-brimmed hat my mother had woven especially for me. Tucking sunglasses in my pocket and wishing myself luck, I rode into the burgeoning dawn.

Few people were out so early and the joggers I passed mostly ignored me. The ride was pleasant and I was thankful for the small number of insects vying to fly into my mouth and up my nose. I gave up rehearsing what might happen if and when I found Ana's place. There were too many unknowns. Instead, I focused on the words of a favorite song, singing it over and over in my head as my legs pushed the pedals round and round.

It took longer than I guessed to reach Ana's house, but as I approached the matching street number there was no doubt which one it was, the edible landscaping apparent to my newly trained eyes. Fragrant and colorful flowers snaked along the ground, creeping up and over gates and trellises. Ana's small yard was more beautiful than any park I'd ever seen. I'm not sure what I was expecting, but I think I had in mind a crime scene like at Clare's. A dug-up yard, boarded windows, yellow tape. A look of vacancy, maybe. After all, it had been a few weeks since Ana had supposedly gone missing. But this place flourished.

I glanced around nervously as I walked my bike up the stone-scattered driveway. Why did I feel like Hansel and Gretel reaching for the shingles of the candy house? I rapped tentatively on the front door, then seeing the button, rang the doorbell. I waited a few moments and was about to turn away when I heard a familiar voice call out.

"Yes, yes. I'm coming, I'm coming."

The door opened, and there she stood. Ana.

"Lily?"

The look of amazement on her face was startling. My heart skipped a beat.

"Ana?"

We stood dumb, staring. Finally Ana moved. She stepped out of the doorway and peered around.

"Just you? Where are Clare and Dante? I can't believe it," she said. "It's so good to see you. But—"

The stipulation Ana had given us about using the map was clear: don't—unless something happens.

"What's happened, Lily?" She pulled me into her house. "Please, sit down."

I sat. Ana looked at me, waiting for an answer, an explanation to my presence. I was still in a daze at finding her here, alive and well, everything normal. Ana, in front of me in her cute little house, not missing at all.

I looked around. Did she just ask me about Clare and Dante? They weren't here with her?

"Lily," she repeated, "what's wrong?"

It was then I noticed how much thinner Ana was, that she used a cane as she crossed the room. A walker stood in the corner.

"I, I didn't think I'd find you here." Even as I spoke, my mind raced, trying to fit the new information into place—bits and pieces, past and present. Maybe she'd seen Clare and Dante, maybe everything was fine.

"Clare was worried when you missed church." I heard my words as if someone else was speaking. In the conversation running just ahead in my imagination, Ana was laughing and saying, *Oh yes, I know, she and Dante told me—after the GRIM agents raided their home. We thought it better for them to stay here for awhile. But things have calmed down, that's why they rode into town today to get you. Where did you say they are now?*

"Lily? Lily—are you okay?" Ana's real voice broke through the imagined one I'd been listening to.

"Did you hear me, child?"

"No, sorry," I mumbled. "I was thinking about something else."

"I must get you something to drink," Ana said, grasping her cane to pull herself up.

"Oh, no," I replied, jumping up. "You stay, I can help myself."

I scrambled to the kitchen, glad to get away and collect myself. I surveyed my surroundings: a shiny white kitchen table with four black chairs, a larger than ordinary stove, a refrigerator, a big double sink, a smooth black counter dotted with an array of glass jars and wooden boxes.

"The cupboard to the right of the sink," Ana called.

I filled my glass from the tap, urging myself to calm down. I drank it slowly before returning to the living room.

"Very well, Lily. Where do we start?"

"Clare and Dante are gone," I blurted. "No one knows where they are!"

3

WHAT HAPPENED TO ANA

"Clare and Dante are missing?"

"Yes." I stifled the would-be sobs into a few sniffles. "They ran away after the police and GRIM agents raided their apartment and put their mom in jail. I've been trying to figure everything out. Ana, didn't you hear about it on the Monitor?" I glanced around the tidy living room. Unlike most places with a Monitor as large as a window, this room hadn't any.

"As you can see, my dear, I don't own a Monitor. I occasionally use one at the library or the senior center when I'm in town, but I prefer not having one in my home. Too many people have stopped living their lives and do everything virtually. But tell me, what happened?" She leaned in closer, searching my face.

"They accused Clare and Dante's mom of growing illegal plants. They took our tomato and pulled up the carrots. But they didn't find any seeds or other things to implicate Celia as a Seed Saver. She kept denying everything, so they let her go. Clare and Dante were gone by then. You haven't heard from them?"

Ana shook her head.

"Where were you, Ana? Why weren't you in church? Clare thought maybe GRIM got you."

Ana nodded toward the walker. "I fell and broke my hip. I was in the care center for a time. I thought Clare would hear about it in church."

"She missed a Sunday," I murmured.

"Do you think it's why they ran?" Ana asked.

"I don't know," I answered. "But, yeah, maybe. Maybe partly you disappearing and then Celia getting arrested." The long-haired cat nestled in Ana's lap accused me with its golden eyes.

"Oh, dear. How long have they been gone? You must tell me everything."

I told Ana what I knew. Oddly, she was concerned about *me*. Had I seen GRIM agents following me, she wanted to know. Did the police question *me*? What did they say to my mother? I assured her I wasn't the one in trouble and suggested we focus on Clare and Dante.

"Clare's mom doesn't have any idea why they ran away," I added. "She's really sad. She looks terrible. Should I tell her what I know?"

Ana didn't answer right away. At last she spoke.

"What do you think, Lily? Can she handle it? Would Celia be supportive enough of the Movement not to jeopardize it?"

I thought about Celia, how she sometimes preferred to be kept in the dark about things. And of my mother and how lost she would be if anything happened to me. Then I remembered Celia's attitude toward the authorities and the story Clare told us about her mom facing down the GRIM agents.

"Yes. She can be trusted," I said. "Celia won't rat us out. It might be hard to keep her in one place if she knew where Clare and Dante went, but if we tell her everything, she won't let us down."

"Okay," Ana said. "In my experience that hasn't always been the case. Seed Savers must possess strong spirits. You may tell her what's been happening. Give as little information as possible. She needn't know my name."

With that, Ana asked for one more thing. She gave me instructions on how to send a coded alert about Clare and Dante out on the Network. I was to use a Monitor in a public location and make sure no one was watching. Afterwards, I had to destroy the instructions and the code. It was a limited, one-way interaction.

Before the sun set, I had accomplished my mission.

4

RED-HAIRED ROSE

I didn't get into too much trouble with my mom for leaving like I did. But it caused an awkward situation: Ma insisted on meeting Rose and her family.

I only knew one person named Rose. I had met her at after-school tutoring earlier in the year. We weren't exactly friends, but I figured if I could find her she would be more than willing to hang out. She was that sort of kid, a regular third wheel. Why her name popped into my head the morning I visited Ana, I didn't have a clue. But my fate was sealed. Once Ma got an idea in her head there was no stopping her. I needed to find Rose and get chummy fast.

It was supposed to be sweltering hot all week, so I got up early to ride around while the weather was cool.

I ached to water my outlaw veggies, but hoped instead Mother Nature would soon oblige. I kept my eyes open for Rose. How on earth was I going to find her?

I rode slowly past a vacant lot where some of my vegetables grew. Because it was early in the day the bean leaves looked strong and fresh though I knew by afternoon they'd be wilted. The first time I'd observed the sad, soft, nearly melted look of wilting veggies, I'd rushed off for water, convinced my babies were on their deathbeds. Over time I'd learned that a little wilt in the heat of the day was to be expected.

Next, I headed for my park plantings, watching for Rose in every yard and driveway I passed. I felt like a peeping Tom. I even went out of my way to glide by St. Vincent's where we'd attended tutoring. By then I realized how unlikely it was I'd ever find Rose, and that I'd need to devise some other way out of the dilemma with Ma. *How could you be so dumb?* I asked myself as I peddled back home.

At the apartment I ate lunch with Ma—a tray of the usual balanced food: Vitees, Proteins, and Carbos. I'm not sure why she made me sit at a table to eat with her— it's not like families sat together for meals anymore. Most kids ate while watching the Monitor. Sometimes Ma was so old-fashioned. I often wondered what she would think of the whole "plant seeds/grow your own food" thing with which I was involved. I thought she'd like it, but I remembered Ana's words, *Seed Savers must be strong.* Not exactly my idea of Ma. She was more the fragile type.

So there we sat, eating our packets together. Less than a day had passed and already Ma was hinting again about meeting Rose.

"Ma, Rose and her family went away for a few days," I fibbed.

"Oh, that's too bad. At least they invite you for the day trip."

"Yes, Ma," I squelched the urge to roll my eyes.

She smiled at me politely. What was it about Asians that made them so polite? It might be a stereotype, but it sure fit Ma. Either way, it hadn't rubbed off on me. Then again, maybe I took after my pop.

I never knew my dad, and my mom didn't talk about him. When I was little I told everyone I didn't have a father. Eventually I discovered it wasn't biologically possible. But when I asked Ma about it, all she said was, "Lily, your father is no longer with us. Do not speak it again." She was so serious and pained-looking that I'd only ever mentioned it twice. I figured my dad had died a tragic death. In the story I imagined, my parents had a wild and romantic courtship and loved each other deeply. I was the sole product of that love before my dad was ruthlessly taken from us. My mother, heartbroken, could never talk about it.

James David Gardener. That's all I knew about my dad. I loved him immensely.

"I'm going to the fountain at the park," I told Ma. "Maybe I can cool off." The too-hot afternoons dragged by without Clare and Dante.

"Be careful."

"You be careful yourself," I teased. She smiled sheepishly and waved me off.

The park was awash in people, twice as many as had been there earlier. They were crowded together in one of two places: the shade of the grand maples or splashing in the fountain. The city had closed its last public pool years before I was born, so park fountains were the best most of us could do on scorchers like today. Sometimes I figured it was a miracle the fountains were still open.

I stayed under the trees at first, but the water teased me like an advertisement. Not one to hold back, I finally let my bike lie, kicked off my flip flops, and rushed into the crowd. The water was cold, but cold was what I needed. I closed my eyes and bent my head back, letting the spray from the fountain pound my upturned face. That's when I heard it—the overly loud voice that had often annoyed me at tutoring: the voice of red-haired Rose.

I opened my eyes and scanned the area. Sure enough, there she was, bossing around three younger kids like she owned the place. What luck! I'd found her now without even trying. I edged my way through the throng, wondering if Rose would remember me and planning just what I'd say. I needn't have worried. While I was yet four and a half meters away, Rose whipped around intent on chastising one of her little friends—or charges—I wasn't sure which, when her eyes glanced over me, then ricocheted back.

"Hey," she called, "what's up?"

I turned and looked behind me.

"I'm talkin' to you."

I smiled weakly. "Oh, uh, nothin'."

Rose abandoned the small children and was standing next to me in a flash.

"What about them?" I asked.

"Just kids. Don't really know 'em. What's yer name . . . Lavender?"

"Lily," I said.

"Yeah—I knew it was a flower—like me."

She smiled then, and for the first time it occurred to me that Rose was pretty. Her red hair was overly fluffy and wild, but her features were nice: a delicate nose and bright green eyes stippled with golden flecks and creamy skin with just enough freckles to be interesting. The smile helped me see what her previous scowls had hidden, the way sunshine illuminates a snow-covered mountain from out of the shadows.

"Right," I said. "You're Rose."

Obviously pleased and impressed that I remembered

her name, she tagged me and laughed and then darted away. We ran around and splashed until we were soaked and out of breath. Rose was more fun than I'd anticipated. Asking her back to my place would be a breeze.

"Can you come over to my apartment?" I asked as we sat on the edge of the fountain, flapping our feet up and down in the water.

"Now?"

"Yeah, sure."

"Where do you live?"

"Ferndale Apartments."

"Off Dixon?"

"Yeah."

"You on your bike?"

"Yeah, it's over there," I said, motioning to where it lay. Several other bikes were piled next to it.

"Me too," Rose said. "Let's ride around 'til we're dry. Your folks home?"

"My mom."

Oh shoot. It dawned on me that my mom might mention to Rose how nice it was that her family had taken me on the fake outing. Not to mention that I'd just told Ma they were out of town.

"Oh no," I said dramatically.

"What?"

"I just remembered, my mom isn't feeling well. Sorry. I can't have you over after all."

"That's okay. No biggie."

We sat splashing our feet a few more moments.

"Lily?"

"Yes?"

"I heard about your friends."

I didn't say anything.

"Have you found out anything new? Like, does anyone know what happened?"

"No."

"I guess you must be worried . . . "

I didn't want to talk about it. I barely knew Rose. All I'd been thinking about every spare minute was Clare and Dante and where they might be and whether or not they were all right. I certainly didn't need snoopy old Rose bringing it up when I had ceased dwelling on it for two seconds. I stared at her with my mouth closed tightly.

My silence achieved the desired effect; Rose dropped the subject.

Suddenly she launched like a rocket running head-on into the fray, screaming as she ran. Rose certainly had an energy new to me. I wondered then and there if this might be the beginning of a strange new friendship.

5

PLAN OF ACTION

When I figured my mom might be worried, I headed home. The apartment was steamy hot even with fans. I played some Monitor games, then watched a few shows together with Ma. Finally it grew late enough to leave Ma and go to my room. Once more, I needed a plan.

I would make a list. It always helped to write things down. The reason I had vegetables growing all over town was because I'd first drawn it on paper. To put ink to paper was to begin. And yet it bothered Ma that I wrote. "Is that schoolwork?" she'd ask if she saw me writing. If I said no, she scowled or chastised me. "Why you always writing? Too much writing not so good." I didn't argue. I just learned to do it behind closed doors.

Plan of Action:

1. Visit Ana again.
2. Start working on Ma about not grilling Rose, or alternately, consider telling Rose about the lie—hmm, but then Rose might want to know where I really was.
3. (More pleasant) Check vegetables. Read and memorize from the gardening books. New idea: Ask Ana if I can see her garden or her books. (Should that be #4?)

This last idea thrilled me. When I had visited Ana I hadn't asked to see what she was growing or if she had more books. We had both been surprised at seeing each other and focused on Clare and Dante's disappearance. It now occurred to me that Ana's house must hold a wealth of resources.

But what about GRIM? Always in the back of my mind I worried. Whenever I went out, I watched for suspicious-looking characters. It didn't *seem* like I was being followed. Ana had asked about agents, made me promise to be on guard, but had not forbidden me from visiting. In fact, we had made plans to meet again. I squelched my worries.

I thought back to the day Clare first showed the two tiny seeds to Dante and me. *These seeds will change the world,* she said. I remembered thinking how overly dramatic she was, yet trusting her just the same; any doubts I ever had about Clare never lasted long. I recalled what had happened a few days later—Clare explaining about GRIM and how she had been followed. Her mother visited by two men in shades and suits. We had been a little scared at first, but over time eluding the men had become a game to us.

I thought about the day Clare introduced us to Ana and how Ana had taught us about seeds and gardening. But Ana had not known the agents followed us. When she found out, she stopped the classes. She told us about Seed Savers and her involvement with the underground movement.

I didn't regret that Ana had taught us. Even now, with Clare and Dante's disappearance, I was glad we had learned to garden, to grow food. Before Ana and her classes about seeds and plants and real food, what had my life been? School, Monitor, folding paper birds, chores. Now I had purpose. Daily, I checked on the progress of *living organisms*. Plants I knew intimately— peas, carrots, lettuce. Friends I'd grown and nurtured from tiny seeds. I knew I would learn more, do more. Someday, I would meet other Seed Savers. Someday, we would move the country back in the right direction. Besides, I was confident that Clare and Dante were okay. To be honest I was a little jealous of the adventure I felt sure they were having.

I ended my list with the thing I needed to do first:

I had to tell Celia what was happening. Though I knew telling her was a good thing for her sake, I wasn't sure how to break it to her. How do you tell a parent that her children are involved in an illegal activity and are essentially fugitives?

Buck up, Lily, I said to myself. *Clare and Dante had to be brave. You can be too.* And with that helpful advice I closed my journal and got ready for bed.

6

GUILT

The morning erupted bright and clear, though by midafternoon clouds swept in by cool breezes darkened the sky like a curtain closing over the end of a play. A welcome relief from August's heat.

I couldn't relax knowing what lay ahead. Celia wouldn't be home until four o'clock. Over and over in my mind I practiced how the visit might go. *Oh Lily, honey, come on in. How are you? I miss my babies,* she would say. *Celia,* I would answer, *I have something to tell you.* On and on it flowed, this conversation in my head, until I thought my brain might shatter.

I stayed in my room as long as I could, then wandered around the apartment. *I want to cook,* I thought. *I want to measure and chop and sauté.* I'd been studying one of the cookbooks Ana had given us, looking up words I didn't know. Cooking sounded fun and like a great way to ease my mind of troubles. Why had everything changed? I cleaned the toilet instead.

To say things didn't go well with Clare's mom would be an understatement. Celia freaked.

"You think what??? You did what??? Let me get this straight: behind my back, under my nose, you children planted seeds and grew vegetables? People don't do that, Lily. It's against the law." She said the last three words with extra clarity and emphasis: *against the law.* Her eyes flashed as a new thought registered. "Someone must have helped you."

I cautiously told Celia about the after-school sessions but refused to give Ana's name. For a moment I feared I'd made a mistake telling her, but only for a moment. Looking back, I can't blame her for the outburst. I only blame myself in not imagining her reaction more realistically.

By the time I left two hours later, I felt better knowing Celia understood why her children had gone away and that she was not to blame. I told her about the message sent to the Network and that she could trust a larger village of friends to look out for her kids. I shared with her Clare and Dante's strong faith.

"They're good kids," she said, tears filling her eyes. "They done a lot with the little they been given."

I promised Celia I'd let her know if I discovered anything new. She understood I considered myself a part of the Movement and that my mother was not to find out.

Later, when I retrieved my journal from under the bed, I made a check mark next to "tell Celia," and surveyed the other things on the list: Ana, Rose, vegetables. Maybe I could accomplish all three tomorrow. With the hard part out of the way, life was looking up.

I began sowing the seeds of motherly discomfort early the next morning. I figured I might as well get a head start.

"Ma," I said over breakfast squares, "I want you to meet Rose but I don't want you asking her a bunch of questions. Kids our age . . . like to be left alone."

To my surprise Ma didn't look hurt. I kept talking. "So anyway, is it okay if she comes over sometime?"

"Of course, Lily. I know you are lonely without—"

She stopped abruptly. I felt my temper rise.

"*Clare*, Ma, without *Clare*. You can say her name. She'll be back. Clare and Dante will come back." I was up and moving fast to my room, slamming the door behind me.

She didn't follow me. I grabbed my journal and began pouring out my feelings. I had overreacted and now I felt guilty about storming off and slamming the door, but I was too embarrassed to return.

Instead, I turned to my list and thought about how to combine the remaining items. If I could pull off Rose meeting my mom, could I continue to use Rose as an alibi while visiting Ana? It seemed so simple, but the deception bothered me. On the other hand, hadn't I been fooling Ma for months while Ana taught us about gardening?

It occurred to me now that if Rose came to Ana's with me, I wouldn't be lying at all. I'd be totally in the clear. But the thought made me uneasy. Visiting Ana would be for the purpose of learning gardening, and bringing in a new person was no small matter. It was an interesting idea, though. I jotted it down to ponder later.

My emotions now scrawled in blue ink across the lined paper combined with the diversion of my plotting made me feel better.

It was still early, the best time for visiting my scattered orphan plants. I kissed Ma as I passed by, indicating all was forgiven. She looked penitent and I knew my outburst, though unplanned, had worked in my favor.

Cool air whipped my face as I ventured up and down the streets on my bike peering at the places concealing my renegade veggies. The milder weather would be a relief for my vegetable friends, as would the bottles of water bulging in my backpack.

These plants, the guilty secret I'd kept from Clare and Dante. I couldn't help myself and yet I felt like a liar and a cheat, never mustering the nerve to confess before Clare and Dante's sudden disappearance. God knows I wanted to . . . Like any deception, it started small. *I'll just plant a few of these here,* I said to myself. *Maybe nothing will come up. I'll tell them if and when a seed actually sprouts.* Then later on, *I'll tell them once I know it's going to survive.* And on and on. The longer I procrastinated and rationalized, the bigger the deception grew—in my case—literally. By early June I nibbled delicate, round, sweet peas and tangy, red radishes. There had been days I couldn't bear to be around Clare and Dante in my deceit.

I'd be in denial if I said I only missed and envied my vanished friends; a heavy dose of guilt haunted me as well. I was the real lawbreaker. I'm the one GRIM should have been watching most carefully.

I emptied the last of my water on the herbs. Despite my planting frenzy earlier in the season, I was disappointed many of the seeds I'd sown yielded plants I couldn't use. Although the lettuces and chards grew like crazy, they didn't taste like much. From my research I learned there needed to be further preparation such as oil for dressing or frying. But how could I do that? Even if I had what was needed, Ma would certainly freak if I started cooking or showed up with a bowl of green leaves for lunch. The herbs—parsley, dill, and so on— had exotic scents, but my understanding was they were used to flavor other food.

Sometimes it seemed that growing and preparing

your own food was indeed time-consuming and complicated, and it was no wonder the old ways had died out.

As I pedaled home, I thought about Ana and all I might still learn from her. My thought bubble burst, however, as I steered my bicycle into our apartment complex and there, riding around in circles, was Rose.

"Hey," she yelled, "there you are."

"How do you know where I live?"

"You told me, Einstein, remember?"

So I had, that day at the fountain.

"Is your mom feeling better?"

I hoped she didn't see the initial look of confusion that skipped across my face before I remembered the fib I'd told. This dishonesty business was hard work.

"Yeah, sure," I managed. "I think she was tired or overworked or something." Rose wasn't really listening to my answer.

"Wanna do something?" she asked.

"Okay," I said. "What?"

"I don't know."

"Monitor games?"

"I'm bored with Monitor games. I do that all the time."

"Do you have brothers and sisters, Rose?"

"A younger sister—I get tired of looking after her— that's why I sneak away when I can," she said, green eyes sparkling and a wide smile peeling open her face.

31

"Wanna ride?" A plan was hatching in my conniving head. Maybe we could ride out past Ana's and see if everything looked okay. Whenever I was out I watched for suspicious people, but honestly, it seemed like GRIM had left with Clare and Dante. Maybe there was also a subconscious tempting of fate, as in, *what more could possibly happen?* After all, my two best friends had already disappeared. Perhaps tempting fate was all that was left.

"Course," Rose replied, darting away.

Rose sped down the block and then to the park where we'd met. We used up and spit out the decrepit bike lanes, then buzzed through the part set aside for skateboarders, much to their ire. Rose stayed in the lead the entire time. I had to hand it to her—the girl had stamina. At last she stopped and I pulled alongside her.

"I'm hungry," she announced.

"Yeah, it's probably time for lunch."

"Lunch? You mean you've already eaten today?"

"You mean you haven't?" I looked at Rose, noticing for the first time her unkempt appearance.

"We don't eat as much in the summer," she stated matter-of-factly. "The schools only serve lunch during certain weeks and no breakfasts after June. My stepmom and dad try to save money."

I wanted to say, *what about the Food Trucks, what about government ration tickets,* but it seemed nosy. It seemed embarrassing. I said nothing.

"So," she said. "Wanna see what pack is on today at Obama?"

Obama Elementary, apparently, hosted one of the free summer lunch programs in my neighborhood. I had no idea about this. My friends and I weren't rich, but we also never ate free community meals.

"Um," I faltered. "Wanna come back to my place?"

7

INTRODUCTIONS

"Rose, how nice to meet you," my mom gushed. Rose shot me a raised eyebrow at Ma's overdone excitement but said nothing.

We ate our choice of lunch combo packs—a balance of Vitees, Carbos, and Proteins. Ma even gave us Sweeties, for which I generally had to wait until midafternoon. She did well in not asking too many questions.

I can't say the same for Rose, but at least she kept quiet in front of my mother. "What's your mom's name?" she asked as we walked to our bicycles.

"Junko."

"Junko? Is she Chinese?"

"Japanese." I said it sort of icily, but Rose wasn't adept at the finer points of communication.

"So you're Japanese?"

"Half Japanese. My father is regular American."

"Where's your father?"

We stood next to our bikes. "Where are we going now?" I asked, avoiding the question.

"I don't know," she answered. "How 'bout you lead this time?"

I hopped on and began riding. I looked around for any sign of GRIM. Rose noticed my gawking.

"Watcha looking for?"

"Spies," I said, overdramatically.

"Oh," she said. "Right." Rose peered around, catching on to what she viewed as a silly make-believe game. "The coast is clear," she sang out.

As we continued riding, I began to lead us toward the edge of town, out toward Ana's. It wasn't long before Rose called from behind.

"Lily, hold up."

I stopped.

"Where are we going?" she asked as she slid in and pulled to a stop beside me.

"Just riding."

"I never leave town."

"It's okay," I said. "I've gone this way; it's not that bad. I don't go too far. Want to?"

"Okay," she said. "It's better with two."

After about twenty minutes I realized it was quite a distance to Ana's—how had I forgotten? It wasn't a good idea to drag Rose out there just yet. I called to her that when the traffic was right we would do a U-turn and head back.

In town we rode straight for the fountain to cool off. "That was great," Rose said. "Really invigorating."

I smiled. It *had* felt good. Maybe this was how to do it. A few times a week ride out of town with Rose, gradually going farther and farther until at last we'd reach Ana's house.

Rose latched on to me like an infant's grasp around your thumb. Every day just after lunchtime she showed up to ride. She seemed to enjoy the "spy" game, always peering about, then calling out "the coast is clear."

Within two days we made it to Ana's house. I had planned to buzz by and turn around, maybe do a little rubbernecking as we passed by; as luck would have it Ana was tottering around out in the blazing sun. And she waved.

I hit my brakes. Rose stopped next to me. Before Rose could open her mouth, Ana spoke.

"Lily? Is that you? And Rose?"

I wasn't sure how to proceed. Act like it was a coincidence for Rose's benefit?

"Oh, hi," Rose answered. "Ana, right? Hey, Lily, it's the lady from St. Vincent's, remember?"

Ana and I exchanged glances.

"Very nice to see you again, Lily," Ana said. "How

wonderful to see both of you. Won't you come inside for a few moments? I'm afraid I've been out in the sun too long."

Rose shrugged her shoulders and looked at me. "Okay by me. What do you think?"

"I could use a break," I said.

Once inside and seated at the kitchen table, Ana set tall glasses before us.

"What is this?" asked Rose, screwing up her face in disdain after taking a long drink of the cold liquid.

"Tea," Ana said. "I made it myself. You are probably used to a much sweeter tea."

"Yeah," said Rose, drinking it anyway. "What do you mean you made it yourself? Like with powder?"

Maybe I wouldn't have to make the important decisions. Maybe Ana was taking the lead.

"As it happens, Rose, tea is made quite easily with just water and leaves—or flowers—from certain plants."

Rose's eyes narrowed and her forehead wrinkled. "What? You made this tea from plants?"

Ana smiled. "Yes, of course, dear. Even the tea and tea mixes from Stores have a plant base. But tea isn't hard to make, so I make my own."

"How?" asked Rose.

"Once you have the leaves, you boil water, pour it over, let it set a spell, then drink. The leaves can be fresh or dried. That's all there is to it. But most folks like it sweet. That's what you're used to. Lots of sugar."

I wondered what Rose was thinking. Ana's explanation had maintained Rose's attention as few things did. Hanging around her in recent days I realized Rose listened to only about half of what anybody said. I didn't know if it was bad manners or if her brain moved so quickly she was already heading down the next mental path, leaving behind whatever was being spoken—even if it was an answer to her own question.

"That's interesting," Rose said at last. "It would sure save money to make your own drinks. And if you could enjoy it without sugar. Maybe you can show me how to do that, and which plants."

Ana smiled. "Of course. Now, before you ride back you'll need some sustenance." She stood and crossed the room, pulling Sweeties from a shelf and placing them before us.

We gobbled up the round, chewy sweets and drank more of the chilled tea. It really was good, and very refreshing. I glanced around the kitchen hoping to see evidence of homegrown food, but saw none. *She's being careful*, I thought. *Just because things aren't out in the open doesn't mean they're not here.* Ana's cat, crouched under the table, eyed me dubiously.

"Wow, that was weird, wasn't it?" Rose said as we mounted our bikes to leave.

"What?"

"Finding Ana out here like that. The way she waved, recognizing us so easily. Strange."

I tried not to look suspicious, pedaling away perhaps too quickly in an effort to avoid eye contact.

It was a relief when Rose told me later that she couldn't come over for a few days. I desperately needed to talk with Ana alone.

8

"TEACH ME!"

"I see you and Rose are getting along," Ana said after welcoming me into her cozy kitchen the next day. I was falling in love with the place. It reminded me of homey scenes I'd seen on old Monitor shows. Sometimes I daydreamed about cooking on the old stove, or working at the counter preparing food, doing more than cutting the wrappers of plastic-coated packages and heating the carefully shaped contents.

"Yeah," I acknowledged, "she's okay."

"How did things go with Clare and Dante's mom?"

I explained how my conversation with Celia transpired. Ana asked whether or not I had sent out the alert on the Seed Savers Network.

"Oh, good work, Lily," she exclaimed. "You are a true soldier in the Movement."

I blushed at the compliment. "It wasn't so hard," I mumbled.

Inside of me, pressure was building during our small talk, like on a hot, humid day before a rainstorm when you feel you could cut the air into squares with a big knife. I rose from my seat and walked toward the open back door where I stood admiring Ana's charming yard.

"Ana, teach me more!" I burst out unexpectedly. "I want to know everything. I'm not afraid. There's nothing more to lose." Something brushed against my leg. I looked down . . . Mrs. Fluffbottom, Ana's cat, walking away.

Still somewhat fragile, Ana once again used a cane to pull herself up. She hobbled over to me. Standing behind me, Ana placed a hand on my shoulder, her eyes joining my gaze. "Okay, Lily."

I exhaled in relief as Ana stepped past me, and I followed her outside. Rather than grass, the area was covered with chipped wood with a stone path wandering through it. Her yard was truly a garden, bountiful in green plants and bright, colorful flowers.

We toured the yard leisurely, Ana naming each plant and describing a little about it. She showed me chamomile, from which our tea was brewed, and pointed out the tops of underground vegetables—beets, carrots, onions. In the back corner grew a large, leafy plant which she declared "a most brazen act" due to its size, but, she explained, so forgotten nowadays as to be unrecognizable: squash.

Finally, Ana smiled and pointed to the lettuce dancing among the zinnias. "I eat a salad every day for lunch," she said.

Ana told me how she used to do more gardening, in recent years raising plants indoors. I was thrilled to hear this; I really wanted to taste a tomato having lost ours before it ripened. My excitement was short-lived, however, when Ana recounted that she had halted many of her growing activities because of her interaction with us kids. She wanted to protect us.

One of the most exciting things Ana *did* show me though, was right out front: a large bush with small, blue berries. GRIM had not cited her for this bush all those years ago even though the berries were completely edible. They were blueberries. Now there weren't a lot of bushes with berries around, except maybe holly, and everyone knew never to eat holly berries since they were poisonous . . . at least enough to make a person sick . . . I once saw a kid eat a bunch and throw up until I thought he would turn inside out. I suppose it's why it didn't occur to me that berries were edible. Not to mention that a short time ago the idea of eating *any* part of a plant seemed absurd, let alone creepy little berries.

Everyone had heard of blueberry-flavored Sweeties, of course. But that didn't mean anything. You know, like other things people said: What did "hold your horses" have to do with being patient, for example? Or sounding like a "broken record" when you said something too many times . . . What the heck was a broken record?

So when Ana showed me the bush and urged me to try the taut, blue berries, it eased the disappointment I'd experienced about the tomatoes. The blueberries, by the way, were yummier than any Sweetie I'd ever tasted.

After a tour of both the back and front yards, we sat down where we had started—Ana's pleasant kitchen table. Like the old books, Ana's kitchen was a kitchen from the past—a place where food was carefully prepared, preserved, and presented.

"Ana, will you teach me about cooking and preserving?"

"Well—"

"What about Rose?" I interrupted. I told Ana that Rose and I hung out often, and about Ma's relief that I had a new friend. I asked what she thought about opening our secret circle to include Rose.

Ana listened silently until I was completely finished—and then some. I searched her face for an answer.

At last she said, "Let me think it over."

9

LESSON ON HERBS

True to her word, Rose's absence continued for the next two days. I shrewdly neglected to mention this to Ma, taking off shortly after lunch as usual, letting her think what she may. The weather was muggy and a light smog muted the summer sky making it appear cooler than it really was. I rode out to Ana's, eager to learn and glad for more time alone with her.

Ana was on her front porch rocking in a white wicker chair. A floral fragrance pleased my nostrils. Downtown never smelled like this. I realized I was smiling.

"Have you eaten?" Ana asked as I dragged my bicycle up the steps.

"Yes," I answered.

"Well I haven't. You said you'd like to learn how

to prepare food. I thought maybe we could start with a salad."

My heart leaped. This was something I'd been dreaming about. All that lettuce growing around town and not knowing how to make it taste good.

"Okay," I said. "I can always eat more." I followed her in and plopped down in my usual spot at the table. She gave me a look that made me wonder what I'd done wrong.

"Lily, *preparing* food is not the same as *prepared* food. It entails effort."

I jumped up. "Sorry."

"I have already gathered the lettuce from the garden because it's best done before it's too warm outside," Ana explained. "Easier to wash when it's fresh and crisp."

Wash? Of course you would wash food from a garden!

Ana opened her refrigerator and withdrew a bag filled with vibrant green and red lettuce leaves.

"This has already been washed, but let me explain the process. I like to fill the sink with water and submerge every leaf," she said. "Make sure all the little critters float off."

My face betrayed my surprise. "Critters?"

Ana smiled. "Yes, dear. We're not the only ones who appreciate good food. Expect an occasional worm or bug, but don't worry about it. That's why we wash it. Also, sometimes it gets dirty from watering or rain when the soil splashes up."

"But what if we miss a 'critter'?" I persisted.

"Extra protein."

I wasn't sure if this was a joke or if Ana was serious.

Ana continued with her instructions. "After the lettuce is submerged, I often pass each leaf under running water just to be sure, then drop it into my handy salad spinner." She took an ancient plastic contraption out of her dish drainer and showed me how it spun. "This helps remove excess moisture. Now," she said, opening the bag, "for the salad."

Ana drew two plates from her cupboard. She tore up the leaves and placed a small pile on each plate. Opening the fridge again, she pulled out a tube-shaped green vegetable.

"Do you remember this one?" she asked as she held up the vegetable. I strained to remember. Like a foreign language, I found it hard to recall all the new words gardening introduced into my vocabulary.

"Cumber something?"

"Cucumber," Ana said. "They're great in salad. Radishes and tomatoes also dress it up. But I'm afraid I don't have either of those right now. However, I love the flavor of fresh herbs." She opened a drawer and pulled out a large pair of scissors. "Come along."

I followed Ana out the back door, nearly tripping over Mrs. Fluffbottom. Ana wove her way along the stone path, snipping here and there.

"I love a touch of dill," she said. "Basil leaves are

also good. And of course, cilantro. Parsley, chives, mint, whatever you've got and whichever you prefer." Ana looked happy and healthy out among her plants. The herbs tucked in her apron pockets, she walked back toward the house, stopping only to cut off the tip-tops of some green onions. Once inside, Ana didn't even wash the herbs, but simply snipped them over our salads. Just like that—from garden to plate. The fragrance was startling.

After that Ana brought to the table a lovely blue bottle with an ornate stopper. She drizzled a shiny substance over each salad. "A little oil to finish it," she said.

"Oil? Like to fry stovetop packets?" Most people didn't bother with that.

"Yes. Only I've flavored mine. This one is infused with basil. But with the fresh herbs we've added, you could use plain oil and be fine."

Seated now, Ana reached over and took one of my hands in hers. She bowed her head and closed her eyes. I did the same.

"Dear God in heaven, thank you for my special friend, Lily. Thank you for this food to nourish our bodies. Amen."

I felt her hand release mine and somehow remembered that "amen" meant "the end" in prayer language. I opened my eyes. Ana smiled at me and picked up her fork.

"Enjoy."

I watched as Ana slid her fork under the leaves and brought it to her mouth. I followed her lead. If I hadn't already munched on carrots and radishes earlier in the summer, I might not have liked the natural "green" taste of the salad. But since I had, I thoroughly enjoyed it. The intricacies of the flavors reminded me of fireworks. You know, like when the big blue explosion makes you go "ahh," then suddenly off to the left and lower down there's a burst of red, a shooting strand of purple, a loud pop, a bright light. Each new taste—cucumber, dill, onion, basil—a new, exciting, unexpected shower of sparks.

"It's so good."

"Mmm," she said, "yes, it is."

After we finished our salads and set our dishes in the sink, Ana asked me to sit down again. I did so readily, anxious to know what she'd decided about Rose. Every way I played it, it seemed advantageous to have Rose know about Seed Savers. And yet I understood Ana's reluctance. It was risky trusting new people. Could Rose keep her mouth shut? She seemed like the type who might blab the wrong thing to the wrong person.

Unfortunately, Ana seemed in no hurry to discuss the matter.

"Lily, did you bring your notebook?"

I was taken off guard. "My notebook?"

"You told me you wanted to continue learning."

"Oh. Yeah. I . . . um . . . I'm sorry. I forgot," I faltered.

"Well I suppose you are young and have a good

memory," she said. "I have to write down everything. I thought we'd begin with food preservation. I love fresh food," Ana said, "but unless you live in a place with warm, sunny weather and an adequate source of water throughout the year, you won't be able to grow vegetables year-round—at least not outdoors. Do you understand what is meant by growing seasons and when a vegetable is *in season?*"

I nodded. Yes, I thought I understood this. I had read a lot in the books we'd been given, and the experience this spring and summer with my renegade plants had given me first-hand knowledge about each seed's time to shine.

"Let's start with herbs," Ana said. "The best way to preserve herbs is to dry them."

I didn't really understand what she meant, but I nodded to show I was listening.

"Herbs are easy to dry and retain excellent flavor. If you plan on using the leaves, harvest them before the plant flowers. The best time to cut them is midmorning. Give them a good shake to rid them of any friends," she said winking. "No need to wash unless they are visibly dirty or growing near a busy street. If you do wash them, be sure to dry well so they won't mold." She lowered her head and peered at me from above her glasses. "You following, Lily?"

"Yes, I'm fine. Midmorning, don't wash, before they flower," I repeated.

Ana continued. "Tie them in bunches and hang them upside down in a warm, dry place—"

"So cut them long?"

"—yes, cut them long. This old house has a nice attic, so that's where I hang mine. It takes a couple of weeks to dry nicely, maybe longer. They should feel dry and crumbly. Then run your hands up and down the stem to remove the leaves."

She ran her hands down an imaginary stem.

"The leaves can be stored whole or crumbled. Whole leaves preserve the flavor better, but crumbled are easier to store. It's best to keep them out of sunlight."

Ana had gotten up and walked to the counter. She gathered some of the small glass jars and boxes which were neatly labeled and filled with green flakes. "Dried herbs," she said, setting the jars and boxes down in front of me.

"How do you use them?" I asked.

"Well, as you saw today, herbs and spices add flavor. I use these when I cook from scratch. It's harder these days without many ingredients available in Stores, but occasionally I can whip something up that benefits from my herb collection. Of course, dried mint and chamomile make excellent tea."

Ana let out a long sigh. "I suppose I preserve much more than I can use; mostly it's habit these days."

From my perspective, aside from making tea, I couldn't think how the herbs would be any use at all dried up and crispy like that. But I wanted to try my hand at it. I just didn't know how to pull it off at home. Unlike Celia, working many hours every day and night, my mom was almost always home.

"Will we be drying herbs here?" I asked.

"Sure, we can do that."

The question about Rose loomed. I looked at the clock . . . two hours had passed since I left home. I jumped up, realizing that by the time I got back I'd be later than usual.

"Thanks, Ana, I need to get going."

"Lily, I won't be home tomorrow in case you were planning on coming over," Ana called as I opened the door to leave.

"You won't?" I don't know why I was surprised. Of course she had an active life. After all, that was how we had met, with Ana's volunteer work at after-school tutoring.

"I have something to do in town after church. Just thought I'd let you know."

"Yeah, thanks. See you later."

Ten minutes into my ride I realized the question about Rose had not been addressed. Rats! With Ana unavailable tomorrow, when would I have another opportunity to talk to her alone?

And what would I do tomorrow? Now that I was hanging out with Rose, the last week had passed quickly. Tomorrow I'd be on my own . . . no Rose and no Ana.

No Clare, no Dante, whispered that small voice within my heart.

10

"WHO CARES ABOUT THE
STUPID GOVERNMENT?"

I tried sleeping in but it didn't work. The sun appeared
too early, invading my room, rousing me awake.
Though out of bed, an inert depression settled over
me like fog filling a valley. I could tell by the way Ma
watched she knew something was wrong. Thankfully,
she didn't ask. Though it was only morning, just knowing I had no afternoon plans dampened my spirit. At
last I gravitated to my journal. I hadn't written in a few
days. I turned to the last couple of entries. So much
had happened this summer. The disappearance of my
friends, finding Ana, connecting with Rose. These were
exciting and extraordinary things—why did I feel so

glum? If this was what being a teenager was like and my thirteenth birthday rapidly approaching, I wasn't sure I wanted to be one. Why not skip this phase altogether? *If only.*

I scribbled these thoughts in my journal for today's entry, along with my misfortune at having no one to hang out with in the afternoon. In a surprise burst, I also expressed my frustration over Ana's not answering me about Rose. But her stalling had given me time to explore my own feelings: I *wanted* Ana to allow Rose into our circle. I missed Clare and Dante and I wanted to share my gardening adventures with someone again. Despite my initial doubts, I believed Rose could keep a secret.

After reading and writing in my journal I felt better. Reviewing and reflecting on what I'd learned from Ana inspired me to retrieve the books she'd given us and see what I could discover about herbs and how to preserve them. But more and more, I was beginning to feel that learning all there was to know about gardening was like trying to connect the dots on a page as big as the world itself.

Rereading the section on herbs in each book, I discovered that not only could herbs be used for tea and seasoning, they could also be used medicinally and for the pleasure of their fragrance. I wondered which kinds of herbs I had planted and proceeded to review the notes I meticulously kept. A few of the seeds hadn't germinated. I'd had no luck with parsley or lavender, but cilantro, basil, thyme, mint, and oregano had all succeeded, some more vigorously than others. My notes confirmed my guess: the herbs I'd sown were primarily used in cooking.

Next, I checked Ana's books for herb preservation methods. While Ana had taught me about drying, she hadn't mentioned freezing, another method listed. It was an odd thought. You could buy frozen treats, and a few people owned box-sized freezers, but the idea of putting herbs or any other plant in a freezer seemed weird. Ma and I, of course, did not own a freezer.

There had to be more. A person couldn't possibly dry every vegetable, yet it was my understanding that most everything could be preserved. Once again I searched the books, this time looking beyond herbs for anything on preservation. I wondered about the books Clare stashed at her place. I hadn't felt comfortable asking Celia, but I was sure that among the books were some on harvesting and preserving. Now that Celia knew about our activities, asking about the books wouldn't be as hard. I knew where they had been kept—under Dante's bed. I set my sights on visiting Celia.

With morning over and a plan of action in my head, I no longer felt depressed. I cheerily made conversation with Ma over lunch to let her know my moodiness had passed. I even offered to help with the origami, explaining that Rose was busy. Ma was delighted to have my help.

The next day, I was lucky to find Celia home before noon. I think maybe I woke her up, but she was happy to see me.

"Lily, come in! Sit down." Her face was hopeful. "Have you heard from my babies?"

I told her I probably wouldn't hear from them directly, but again assured her that if I did, I'd let her know.

"Celia," I said, "remember how I told you about Clare and Dante and me learning to grow food?" She nodded. "Our teacher gave us some books . . . Were any books taken when the police seized the tomato plant?"

"No," she answered. "Nobody said nothin' bout no books. But the place was tore up real good. It's possible they took things without tellin' me."

"No, not if they were trying to get you in trouble. Do you mind if I look? They were in Dante's room."

"Go ahead."

We walked to the partitioned space that was Dante's room. I got down on my hands and knees and peered under his bed.

Celia grinned. "I don't think even you can crawl under there."

"Let's move it," I suggested.

Back in the farthest corner we found what remained

of our precious books. There were only six; those combined with my four did not equal all of our contraband books. I was certain Clare and Dante had taken some with them.

"They packed books when they ran away? I can't believe it. No, I can. Only my kids would stash books in their knapsack." She shook her head, but her eyes were smiling. "I hope you're right about all those *friends* taking care of them, Lily. 'Cuz they sure can't eat no books, even if they are books about food."

She laughed after she said it, which made me glad.

I wasn't home ten minutes when Rose showed up. I guess she thought being absent a few days earned her an invite to lunch. I'd halfway expected her, though, and in truth, was happy to see her. Ma, of course, was gracious, and I figured if Rose normally ate the free school lunches, she needed every free meal she could scrounge—but I also knew it was a drain on our meager resources.

Over lunch, Rose complained about the days spent watching her sister and doing extra chores while her stepmom was out of town. Her dad worked full-time and usually left the meals, laundry, and other tasks to Jen, her stepmom. Rose had to play backup whenever Jen was sick or had other things to do.

Ma complimented Rose for being such a big help to her family. I was embarrassed, but Rose seemed to appreciate it. You got the feeling no one in her family responded with ample gratitude, so even the slightest approval from Ma was cherished. We take what we can get.

"Ready to ride?" Rose asked before I'd swallowed my last bit of teriyaki-flavored Protein.

"Sure," I said.

We headed in our usual direction. After about twenty minutes, Rose pulled parallel with me. "You think we'll see that old lady again—Ana?"

"Maybe."

"Should we stop or just ride by and look?"

I'd been wondering the same thing. Ana had not answered my question.

"Well?" Rose waited for my answer.

"What do you think?"

"How 'bout we ride slow and if she's out, we stop. If not, we ride by, then stop on the way back."

"Okay," I said. "By then, we could use the break. Even if Ana's not around, we could sit on the grass a few minutes."

Ana's yard was empty. We rode past and turned around at the next bend. On the way back, Rose pulled into the worn driveway and pedaled up to the house, me not far behind. She dropped her bike and galloped onto the porch. She was already banging on the peeling white door before I had leaned my bike against the house. I heard Ana's voice call "coming" from inside. I reached the top step just as the door opened. Rose surprised me with that great smile of hers, the one that turned her into a pretty girl. She shined it brightly at Ana.

"We're here again!"

Ana beamed back at her. "So you are."

Once inside, Ana again offered us iced tea. This time, rather than chamomile, she served mint tea—with some fresh leaves in it. This was very exciting—for me because I was actually growing mint, and for Rose because she was so intrigued with the notion of "home-made" tea.

You can imagine my surprise, however, when Ana turned and asked if I'd remembered my notebook this time.

"I . . . um . . . " I looked at Rose, then Ana, "you know . . . "

Rose looked at me. "Your notebook?" She looked at Ana. "We need notebooks?"

"Lily has, in the past, taken notes on what I've taught her," Ana explained. "I thought you girls were interested in learning how to brew your own tea. Day before yesterday Lily dropped by and I reminded her to bring her notebook."

"Lily, how come you didn't tell me?" Rose asked.

I looked at Ana for help, but her eyes only twinkled with mischief. Could this be her way of answering yes about Rose?

"I'm sorry, Rose, I forgot. You know, we weren't sure we were coming here. Remember?"

"Yeah, that's true," Rose admitted. She turned back to Ana. "So we're going to make tea right now?"

"Do you have time? I wouldn't want to keep you."

Rose and I looked at each other. I checked the time. "Yeah, sure. We're okay." I spoke for both of us.

"Follow me," Ana said.

Ana plucked a straw hat from the top of her refrigerator and pulled the large scissors from the drawer. To my surprise, she hobbled out her front door and across the yard. There, along the edge of her lawn, sat a planter filled with the pointed, green mint leaves. I was surprised I hadn't noticed it before. Herbs were indeed easy to overlook. *They might just be the key to our revolution,* I thought to myself.

"Here we go," Ana said. "Mint is a relentless plant. I try to keep it contained lest it take over the whole yard."

"It smells good!" Rose cried in delight. "It comes like that? I thought only flowers smelled."

Ana and I laughed. It felt good to be sharing the wonder of nature with someone new. Ana cut a fistful of the leafy stems, gave them a good shake, and handed them to Rose. Back inside, Ana let the tap run briefly over the leaves. Then she filled a pot with water and brought it to a boil. She turned the burner off, dropped the mint in, put the lid on, and set a timer for twenty minutes. While we waited, sipping the tea she'd given us earlier, Ana explained what would happen next.

"People who like their tea sweet would add sugar at this point. Some folks say the sugar helps extract the mint flavor from the leaves. I don't care for sweet tea, so I don't do that. After the leaves steep—that's what you call this time of waiting—we'll strain them out. For iced tea, of course, you let the tea cool then keep it in the fridge—if you have one—or serve it with ice like any drink you prefer cold. It's nice to put a fresh mint leaf in the glass when you serve it," Ana added, winking.

"Can you buy sugar, just plain?" Rose asked.

"Actually, you can," Ana answered. "But it's not easy to find since most food and drink products are sold totally prepared."

"I love it," Rose purred, her fingers wrapped tightly around the tall glass of fresh mint tea.

"Be sure and fill Rose in on the details of gardening," Ana told me as we were about to leave. "We wouldn't want her to be uninformed. It is of utmost importance people understand what they are involved with," she said, emphasizing each word and glancing over at Rose as she spoke. I didn't need to ask what she meant. I knew Ana was leaving it to me to impress on Rose the discretion necessary in growing and preparing food. Even talking about something as simple as tea making might lead to trouble with the government. Rose, meanwhile, gave us both a funny look at Ana's wordy salutation.

Midway back, Rose and I stopped to rest in the shade of a large oak tree.

"So you get to teach me about gardening?" Rose asked. "I really like that we can make our own tea," she continued, as I stalled trying to figure out how to say what needed to be said. "This will save us so much money," Rose rattled on. "And it will help conserve the ration tickets, too, if we don't have to buy as many drinks. I wonder, do you think it's healthy?"

I couldn't help rolling my eyes. "The tea? Of course it's healthy. You saw what was in it—water and mint leaves. Rose, there's something you need to know. There's a reason people don't go around making their own Juice and Sweeties and Vitees. It's against the law." There, I said it.

"It is?"

"Yes."

"Why?"

She had me there.

"Why, Lily?"

"I don't really know," I said. I thought back to when it all began. Clare had started this whole thing. She had done the research. I wasn't completely sure why it was against the law.

"I think it has to do with ownership of seeds, or safety."

"Safety?"

"Yeah, something about people dying from food not properly processed."

"Oh. That makes sense. Sooo . . . how about making tea from leaves? Is that illegal?"

When she put it that way, I wasn't even sure. I knew owning seeds and growing plants was illegal, but if you found something already growing and knew it was edible, was that illegal? To collect and use it?

"Um, I'm not sure. Listen, Rose, the important thing is that you don't tell anybody that someone is teaching you about real food and gardening. That's what could get you into trouble. And it would get me into trouble, and Ana. So, it's a secret, okay? If you want to keep learning from Ana, it has to be a secret. You don't need to decide now; you can think about it. But don't tell anyone."

Rose looked at me long and hard, those green eyes drilling fire into me.

"What's there to think about?" she said, almost flippantly. "Of course I want to learn more. Who cares about the stupid government?"

11

LILY TELLS ALL

I had plenty to write in my journal that evening. What an exceptional day! My visit with Celia had gone well, and I now had six more books from which to learn about food and gardening. And the unexpected turn of events concerning Rose and Ana had changed everything. I had a new co-conspirator.

As I wrote, I encountered conflicting emotions. There was happiness and relief—I no longer felt alone. There was also guilt and worry—was I replacing Clare? There was confusion about how much I should share— should I tell Rose about my plants or check with Ana about everything first? Could Rose be trusted?

However, I couldn't deny the current of excitement coursing through me. And while I appreciated Clare's level-headedness and spiritual faith, Rose had a tenacity and abandon that invigorated me.

"Lily?" My mom called from behind my closed door, interrupting my thoughts. "Lily, what you doing in there?"

"Just thinking, Ma."

"Why not think out here?"

There she was, suspicious again of my writing. I already wasn't allowed a Monitor in my room. Obviously I couldn't read gardening books in front of her, and for whatever reason she disliked my journaling. I bristled at my mom's incessant meddling.

"Okay, Ma. Just wanted to write a bit."

I heard her tongue clicking in disapproval as she walked away.

The next morning it was already hot by 10 a.m. I loaded up as much water as I could and tended to my plants. By the time I finished, sweat poured down my face and soaked my clothes. There was no way Rose and I would be able to ride out to Ana's. Ma, too, was watching like a hawk, reminding me to wear a hat, put on sunscreen, blah blah. Her overbearing concern annoyed me; I didn't need her to tell me to stay out of the sun.

Secretly, I hoped Rose wouldn't show up. But she did.

"Wow, is it ever hot out there!" Rose exclaimed as she entered our apartment. "I'm not sure we can go to—"

65

"The park?" I interrupted, afraid Rose was about to spill the beans right there in front of Ma. "Sure we can. We'll get drenched in the fountain. Here, take a water," I offered, handing her a packaged water, wishing we had a freezer or refrigerator so it would be truly cold.

After Ma's routine admonitions about being careful, avoiding heatstroke, etc., Rose and I were out the door.

"Sorry I cut you off in there—"

"I gotcha," she said.

"And yes, it's way too hot to ride to Ana's."

Rose nodded in understanding and then we pedaled hard to get to the shade of the maple trees at the park. Once there, we commiserated about the heat and discussed our recent visit to Ana's house and the wonders of gardening and making tea. One thing led to another and before long I had blabbed the whole story of how Clare first met Ana in church, our subsequent after-school tutoring/gardening classes, Seed Savers, GRIM, all of it.

"Is that what happened to Clare and Dante," Rose gasped. "GRIM got them?"

"No, no," I said. "I'm sure they took off because of GRIM, but GRIM didn't *get them*. It wouldn't make sense. Because I'm still here; Ana's still here. I think Clare panicked when the cops arrested her mom. Somehow she thought it would be better for her mom if they left."

"Have you heard from them?"

"No," I admitted. "Not yet. Ana hasn't told me how to connect with the Seed Savers Network. This is serious stuff, Rose. It feels like I already told you too much."

Rose looked around. I studied her face as she scanned the people at the edge of the fountain, walking down the paths, seated on the benches. A new wariness crept into her eyes and I felt guilty for putting it there.

"Come on, I have something to show you," I said. As long as she knew the whole story I saw no reason to keep my outlaw plants a secret. I jumped up and ran along the path. Next to some bushes, in a place not well-tended by the volunteer staff, I pointed to what might pass for weeds: cilantro, basil, and thyme.

"For tea?" Rose asked.

"No, I don't think for tea. But good for adding flavor to other food dishes."

Rose broke off some leaves and tasted them.

"Interesting."

We went to another place in the park.

"Mint!" Rose cried. I was impressed she remembered. "We can make our own tea, Lily!"

"Shh!" She had spoken too loudly.

We walked back to our bikes, talking in hushed tones. I pointed out the problem with making our own tea—we both lived in apartments where other people were always home.

"What about Clare's place?" Rose suggested. "Didn't

you say you told her mom everything and that she was good with it?"

"You mean ask Celia if we can carry on illegal activities in her home, right after she was busted and jailed for that very thing?" I tried not to sound sarcastic.

"Yeah, okay, so maybe not."

After that, Rose and I played in the fountain until we were good and soaked and several degrees cooler. Then I hopped on my bike and shouted, "Follow me!" We rode to the vacant lots, waysides, and stacked tires where I had planted seeds. I showed Rose places where nothing had grown and places where my plants had flourished. We ended up back at the apartment, completely dry from the heat. Behind the closed doors of my room I shared with Rose my notes, sketches, and books. It was a lot for one day.

After Rose left, butterflies did the tango in my stomach. I hoped I hadn't made a mistake.

12

THE LESSONS CONTINUE

"How are you girls today?" Ana asked as we sat down for tea. "I missed you yesterday, but it was just too hot, wasn't it?"

"We're fine," I said. "And yes, it was too hot." I rolled my eyes for good measure.

"She told me everything," Rose blurted. "Don't worry, I can keep quiet."

Ana's eyes took in all of Rose. You wonder sometimes, about old people, the way they look at you, size you up, but don't say what they're thinking. Some kind of wiseometer.

"Yes, Rose," Ana said at last, "I believe you can."

I swallowed in relief. "Ana, we brought our notebooks today," I said before Rose could say anything more.

"Good, let's get started. Lily, you remember I taught you about drying as a means of preservation?"

I nodded.

"Though drying, or dehydrating, is wonderful for herbs and fruit, it's not as good for vegetables. It can be done, of course, but I never cared for the taste. Freezing was my mother's preferred method."

Rose started to say something but Ana kept talking.

"Freezing is not a viable option for us these days, however, because of storage. The government would be suspicious if an old woman like me had a large freezer using so much power. I freeze what I can, but most of my preservation is canning. It takes a few pieces of special equipment and the knowledge of how to do it, but otherwise it's fairly straightforward and the vegetables last a long, long time."

Ana stood and walked to the counter. She reached into a canvas bag and pulled out two glass jars. One was filled with green beans and another with round, red balls.

"Are those tomatoes?"

"Yes," Ana said. "Canned tomatoes and canned green beans. Listen and take notes while I explain the basics."

Rose and I readied our notebooks. *Preservation: Canning*, I wrote. Rose copied me.

For Rose's sake, Ana reviewed and summarized that if a person grew more than could be eaten fresh there were various ways to preserve the extra for later. She briefly covered drying and freezing—causing us to hurriedly scribble notes on the back side of our page—before going into depth about canning. She reminisced about her mother preserving the harvest each summer and fall. How they rarely bought fruits and vegetables from stores. She said she'd helped her mother with the canning but had not done it herself, and only learned how later on when it was almost illegal.

After that, Ana carefully described the jars, special lids, large pots and "boiling water baths" used for canning. It sounded difficult, and I wondered if I could do it. Could I be so brave to learn how, and then follow through without messing up? If I didn't do things right the food could be toxic.

Ana read my apprehension.

"Don't be afraid, Lily. It isn't so hard. It's just a new thing to learn, like all new things."

For her part, Rose asked a lot of questions, scribbling profusely in her notebook.

After Ana finished our lesson on preservation, I brought up the subject of contacting Clare and Dante. I told her I'd visited Clare's mom again and retrieved the books. I mentioned that Celia would feel better if she knew the kids were okay.

Ana nodded in understanding. "They're okay," she said. "You may tell her they are safe."

"You've talked to them?"

"Not directly, no. I was in town this morning, and I connected with the Network. The children traveled north. They found friends. More tea?" Ana asked.

It was obvious Ana did not want to elaborate. Her bluntness not only kept me from asking more, but even subdued the normally relentless Rose.

"Oh good," I muttered. "I'll let Celia know."

By then it was time to hit the trail. Rose and I thanked Ana for her lessons and lit out toward home.

Not in a hurry to return to her apartment, Rose hung out at my place. Ma was reading her Japanese magazine on her mini-Monitor as she did every afternoon. We settled into my room.

"Let's see those books again," Rose said.

I got out the books, including those I'd recently rescued from beneath Dante's bed.

"I need to learn everything," Rose said. "Show me everything Ana taught you before."

We pawed through them: gardening books, cookbooks, seed saving manuals, the book dedicated solely to preserving.

"So this is how people learned how to do stuff before the Monitor?" Rose said.

"Yeah, I guess."

"I like it," she said. "We don't have many books at our house. And the cheap Monitors always have problems. Too bad they don't teach how to do stuff in school."

"Yeah, school is more about knowledge than life skills. And growing your own food is blocked on the Monitor, anyway," I said.

"I don't get that. What else don't we know about?"

I laughed. "You got that right. I mean, nowadays we don't even know what it is we don't know!"

13

FOLLOWED

ur schedule varied only slightly in the following days. Rose and I spent nearly every morning tending the edibles I'd grown around the city, and most afternoons we rode out to Ana's.

I suppose it was our camaraderie that caused us to be sloppy and our enthusiasm that got us noticed. Not to mention the too obvious routine of it all. We were as regular as the tide. One day, just after we left the park and were on our way to a vacant lot, Rose took a wrong turn. When I called to her, she yelled back, "Follow me!" and rode off the normal route, dodging into an alley instead.

"What's going on?" I asked when I caught up—part worried, part annoyed.

"We're being watched."

I felt my eyes widen, my mouth drop open. "What? When? Who?"

She shrugged her bony shoulders. "A kid."

"A kid? Rose! You scared me. I thought you meant GRIM, or the police."

"Who says he's not?" She was deadly serious.

"Well . . . I don't know . . . "

"Same kid, last three days. At first he only watched us in the park. Today he started to follow us out of the park. But I lost him pretty easily back there," she said, tilting her head.

I blushed. I hadn't noticed anything. Here I was, the old pro, and it was Rose who was keeping an eye out for enemies.

"What now?" I asked.

"I don't know, I came *here* so we can talk about it."

We had dismounted and were walking our bikes down the lane. A man exited the back door of his house and started banging on an old car in the alley. We climbed back on our bikes and rode until we found a better location to talk—the rear steps of a crumbling elementary school not far from where we had started.

"Well?" Rose asked.

"I don't know," I repeated. "What did he look like?"

"Like this."

We both jumped at the deep, accented voice. A boy of fifteen or sixteen stepped around the edge of the building. He was tall enough, with dark, wavy hair and straight white teeth. Briefly he extended his right hand, then as if on second thought, he pulled it back, sticking both hands deep into the front pockets of his jeans.

"My name is Arturo. You no need to run from me."

Rose was already on her feet. She stepped toward him rather than away.

"Oh yeah, Arturo?" She said his name wrong— Artero—not like he'd said it: Artoorro, with a firm *u* sound and that special trill on the *r*. "Why were you watching us? Seems pretty creepster to me."

Arturo glanced around as if to make sure we were alone.

"I know what you are doing," he whispered. "I grow vegetables too."

Rose backed down, clearly not expecting this answer.

"You do?" I finally managed to say.

"Yes," he said. It sounded like *jess*.

"Where?" demanded Rose.

"My house," he said. "Will you like to see?"

Honestly, I wanted to. There was something about Arturo that made me trust him. But, intuition aside, Lily Gardener is nothing if not rational. First class rule follower. You simply do not go home with strangers.

"Oh, um, not now," I stammered. "We have things to do."

"Yeah," spit Rose, "what she said."

For the life of me, I couldn't figure out why Rose was being so impolite.

I was on my bike already, pushing off, Rose right behind me. "Bye," I said. "Nice to meet you," I added instinctively.

Arturo smiled. "With pleasure."

Rose and I ate lunch at the apartment and though I wanted to talk about Arturo, I didn't dare mention him around Ma. Finally we finished and retreated to my room.

"What did you think of him?" I asked.

"Who?"

"You know, *the guy.*"

"Artero? I guess maybe he's not a GRIM stooge— but he could be, ya know. But I don't think so. I'm not even sure he's 'legal' if you know what I mean."

Of course I knew what she meant. Lots of immigrants sneaked into our country every day. It may not be the paradise it once was, but with global climate change displacing many and the sheer size of the nation, the United States was still a desirable destination.

It was a rude thing for Rose to say. I was seeing a side of her I hadn't yet encountered.

"He seemed nice," I said. "I can't believe he grows vegetables. Rose, what if there are more people who know about real food than we figured? Maybe things *can* change. You know, this is what Ana was preparing

Clare and Dante and me for—for a time when everybody was free to grow their own food *if they wanted to.* I think we should get to know him."

"Yeah, well he'll probably still be creeping on us tomorrow," Rose said disgustedly. "Come on, let's head to Ana's; she said we could cook today."

As promised, Ana showed Rose and me how to prepare food. First we picked the squash—zucchini it was called—and sliced it into thin rounds. Then Ana introduced us to another underground treasure—garlic—which we cut up tiny and stirred quickly in hot oil. The fragrance was strong but pleasing. Next, we added the zucchini to the oil with a pinch of salt and cooked it on high heat until it was browned but not too soft.

At last we sat to eat our first cooked meal of something that had not been wrapped in plastic, sealed in a box, and bought at a Store. I forgot to warn Rose about Ana's custom of praying at meals, but I needn't have worried, Rose caught on right away. I wondered how she knew. Then Rose and I watched Ana for a cue as to how to eat the zucchini.

Ana inhaled deeply. "Smells divine," she said. "I never grow tired of the aroma." She placed a fork-full in her mouth and chewed. "Mmm. Fine job, girls, fine job."

Rose sampled the zucchini without hesitation. She nodded her head. "Good," she declared. "Yeah. I really like the brown edges."

I pushed the zucchini around on my plate for awhile before tasting a tiny bit. It was different. Definitely it was better than the processed Vitees I normally ate. But it wasn't like what I'd eaten so far—the carrots, salad, radishes. It was too soft. Maybe I was just used to my vegetables uncooked.

"Well, Lily?" Ana asked. They were both watching me, waiting for my opinion.

"Um . . . it's good," I said.

They didn't prod. We finished our plates with talk about the weather and lingered over mint tea.

"Thank you so much for teaching us. This is a dream come true. I just wish—no offense," I said, turning to Rose, "I just wish Clare and Dante were here."

"Of course," Ana said.

"Ana, why won't you teach me how to communicate with the Seed Savers Network? Not just sending an alert like before, but to *really communicate*."

A cloud passed over Ana's face. She had avoided the subject ever since I'd first asked. Initially, I thought it was because the process was so complicated. But the more she delayed, the more I believed she was hiding something. I didn't understand what, or why.

"Lily"—she glanced up at the clock—"isn't it time you girls head back?"

I sighed. I was frustrated, but she was right. The cooking lessons had consumed our time as we had consumed the zucchini.

"Yes," I agreed. "We need to go."

"Thanks, Ana." Rose said. "I loved the zucchini!"

"You're welcome, dear."

As we walked to our bikes I wondered why Ana was reluctant to teach me how to communicate with the Network. Was it because of Rose?

I knew I should be patient, but I felt an urgency. What if something happened? Like in the spring when Ana suddenly stopped teaching us, or like when Clare and Dante up and disappeared? I hadn't been taught yet how to actually *save seeds*. There were still so many things to learn. I needed to be able to communicate with the others *just in case*.

14

SECRETS

The next morning Rose didn't show up to ride around and help with the vegetables. I considered staying home. One day wouldn't hurt; if anything needed to be watered or harvested it would wait another day.

But I had anticipated seeing Arturo again and *that* couldn't wait.

My first stop was a vacant lot near our apartment where I had numerous plants, including green beans. The fruit of the plants—long, stringy pods—was growing large and I was sure it needed picking soon. I hesitated, staring at the beans from across the street. What if GRIM were watching? The fact that Rose had noticed Arturo following us while I remained oblivious unnerved me. No, the beans would have to wait until I had a plan.

I crossed the street and walked my bike slowly along the lot, peeking at the various herbs, chards, and lettuce fighting it out among the weeds. The lettuce had grown tall and was forming little blossoms; the leaves seemed smaller than usual, resembling the weeds surrounding it. I sprinkled the wilted vegetables with the water I'd brought, then stepped back and glanced around. No sign of GRIM agents or Arturo. In fact, virtually no one was about, with very little traffic either.

From there, I rode to the park. As unreasonable as it seemed, I felt less conspicuous with my plants in a place filled with people—it didn't look strange wandering around a park as opposed to loitering near vacant lots. And maybe at the park I'd run into Arturo. Perhaps he was already watching.

There was nothing sneaky about him. Arturo was seated on a bench where the pigeons gather, an old man snoozing away on his shoulder. I walked by, trying not to laugh.

"Hi!" Arturo cried out, startling the man awake.

I looked back, surprised he had called. He had jumped up and was beside me in a flash.

"Where is your friend?"

"Uh . . . she didn't show up today. Sometimes she babysits her sister."

He must have sensed my nervousness, as he stepped farther away.

"What is your name?" he asked.

"Lily."

"Lily," he repeated. "I like that. My name is Arturo . . . if you forget."

We kept walking, but the conversation died. Awkward. For all her nastiness, I wished Rose were here. Or better yet, Clare; Clare would have known what to say. Clare had friends who were boys. Me, I didn't know how to be around them. Dante was okay, but he was Clare's little brother—it didn't really count.

"So," Arturo finally said. He didn't say anything more. I listened; I listened really hard. I wanted him to keep talking. Anything.

"So?" I asked.

He whispered, "Do you visit your *jardin* every day?"

I loved the way Arturo talked. A light accent, a grammar error here and there . . . a Spanish pronunciation like *jardin* instead of garden.

"Yeah," I said, "pretty much."

"Me too," he said. "I mean with *mi jardin*, not *your jardin*," he clarified. "Although less, now, in late summer. In the spring, when is beginning—every day. Every day. Even before anything—how you say—before I see anything."

I thought back to when we first planted the carrot seeds outside of Clare's apartment, how we walked by twice a day just to see if anything was sprouting. I nodded. "Yeah, I know what you mean."

"Do you mind," he asked, "if I walk with you as you view your plants?"

My apprehensiveness kicked in. I stopped. "Arturo, you know it's . . ." I searched his face openly for the first time, grasping for the right words, wondering if he knew the trouble I could get into.

"Illegal?" he said.

When he said it, the way he said it, the word meant something more. The tinge in his voice made me realize it was a word that had been used on him, or at least on his people. I looked away, ashamed and embarrassed.

"Yes."

"I am aware," he said.

I was still trying to figure out whether or not he was angry when his voice changed back, softened, lost the edge. "So I can accompany you, or no? I promise we will be careful. I know about the laws."

There wasn't time for me to think. To write. Only the moment.

"Sure," I said.

I don't know how long Arturo had been watching Rose and me, but he knew where all my plants were. I mean *everything*. And he knew *what* everything was. Later that day as I reflected on the morning, I was again amazed at how transparent my gardening had been to anyone paying attention.

After lunch, I headed for Ana's. If Ana had any qualms about teaching me to access the Seed Savers Network in the presence of Rose, today would be an ideal opportunity.

Ana was surprised I was alone.

"Rose?" she asked simply.

"Don't know. Sometimes she doesn't show up. Her family."

"Do you not communicate with her?"

"Like texting?" I asked.

"Whatever it is you kids do these days," Ana said.

"No. Most of that stuff is too expensive or doesn't work so good. I don't like carrying a telecom." I shrugged. "We just find each other."

Ana and I were sitting at our usual spots in the kitchen. As always, she had set a glass of tea before me.

"Lily, why are you so intent on learning how to connect with the Network?"

"So I can communicate with Clare! And you know, the others—just in case." I felt too ashamed to finish the sentence. Like it was bad luck to mention the possibility of anything bad happening.

"Clare and Dante are not on the Network. It's too risky."

This surprised me, but I couldn't think of anything to say.

"There's a reason I haven't told you everything," Ana continued. "I shouldn't even be allowing you to visit my home. It was just so good to have company." She sighed. "But that's selfish of me."

What? Her words seemed unduly harsh.

"Where does your mother think you are now?"

Why is she asking me this? "With Rose, riding bikes," I answered.

"Have you ever spoken to your mother about gardening?"

I recalled the time earlier in the year when I learned what my last name—Gardener—meant. How I couldn't help myself—I'd gone home and told Ma all about it. She had listened in a cold silence and when I'd finished talking said only, "That is true, but there are no such things as gardeners anymore. Our food comes from Stores. Farmers work for the government. Forget Gardener. It is only a name, like Goldsmith. We have jewelers now, not goldsmiths. Only a name."

I had been hurt and never broached the subject again. The topics my mother and I never spoke of were vast, like so many objects locked in an attic or buried deep in a basement.

"No," I told Ana, "not really. My mom is very . . . law-abiding." I couldn't hide the bitterness seeping into my voice.

"Lily, dear, I'm so sorry. I haven't been open with you."

The intensity of Ana's eyes made me uncomfortable.

"When Clare first brought you to tutoring, I could tell just by looking at you that you were James's little girl. I didn't need to hear your last name. But what could I do? Tell Clare you were not welcome?"

Did she just say "James's little girl?" Ana knew my father? "What?"

"I said, what could I do? I couldn't tell Clare she wasn't welcome to bring her best friend." Ana smiled.

"Why wasn't I welcome? You knew my father?"

"Oh, Lily. What does your mother tell you about your dad?"

"Not much. Wait, *you knew* my father—how did you know my father?"

"Your father, James Gardener, was a leader in the Seed Savers Movement."

I gasped. *What? My father? How could this be?* Ana continued speaking as I listened silently, too shocked to speak.

"About fifteen years ago, before you were born, your dad was instrumental in unifying groups around the country who wanted to change government policy on seed ownership, gardening, food laws, and so on."

"He was?" I managed to squeak out.

Ana nodded. "When the new food regulations were first implemented and most people ate only the overly processed food, a contingent persisted in fighting for *real food*. They fought the ordinances and staged protests. But the sit-ins and food freedom marches were a mere bother the government didn't take seriously. The demonstrations died as people tired and lost hope of making a difference."

Ana smiled, perking up. She had a far away look in her eyes.

"Your father was just coming of age when the protests garnered massive news coverage. It was before the Monitor was reined in—back in the "wild west" days of social media when anyone and everyone could communicate instantly around the world. Do you even know about that, Lily? Have you any idea how easy it once was?"

Ana tilted her head to the side, waiting for an answer. I shrugged. I didn't really understand. Though the Monitor was pervasive in everyday life, it wasn't in the interactive, real-time sense she suggested. These days special licensing was required to engage heavily in two-way Monitor transactions. I suspected this was one reason Ana was hesitant about teaching me—because it would undoubtedly involve more illegal activity.

"Anyway," Ana continued, "your dad was about your age when the final nail in the coffin of food freedom was pounded in. Seed ownership was officially banned, along with growing food without government authorization. Though your dad's family had never gardened, his grandparents had, and young James grew up enjoying rare, homegrown, home cooked meals every holiday. He watched intently the news coverage of protests around the country and wished he could be a part of it. It made a lasting impression on him."

Ana smiled again, pausing. I was listening eagerly, captivated to learn anything about my father.

"Ten, fifteen years later, your dad found himself at the forefront of a movement that had gained strength underground. His skill as a writer united thousands of protesters into a group eventually becoming known as Seed Savers."

I was stunned: my father helped start Seed Savers? Suddenly my mind shot to my mother. My quiet, hardworking, innocent mom. Where was she in all of this? Before I could speak, Ana continued.

"After social media was regulated and communication regressed, your father began writing an underground newspaper. It was distributed the old-fashioned way—by hand—and since GRIM hadn't thought anyone would go to the trouble, it spread swiftly across the country under their radar. A new, stronger movement emerged."

As Ana talked on, terror and fear gripped me. I could feel the cold, white fingers wrapping around my heart. How had my father died? What had happened?

"Stop!"

Ana was visibly startled. So was I. I hadn't realized I'd spoken. My hands covered my ears. Ana remained silent for a minute or two.

"Lily?" she finally said.

I let my hands fall to my lap. "It's too much," I stammered. "Too much all at once. I . . . I . . . need to leave."

Without saying goodbye, I got up and ran out. I walked my bike a good half mile before climbing on. I walked because I was crying too hard to see well. This story Ana had told me . . . how could I make sense of it?

When I eventually arrived home, I had gained the necessary time and distance to be able to stride into the apartment and greet my mother with a straight face. I took a long drink of water and headed to my room. This would require a lot of writing.

15

A RESURRECTION OF SORTS

I didn't leave the apartment on Wednesday. Though grateful Rose hadn't shown up, I was also slightly worried. Had something happened? My brain, however, had too much vying for its attention to give more than a passing thought to my missing friend.

What was I going to do about the information I'd learned about my parents? Should I confront my mom? No, I needed to hear the rest of the story. And as difficult as it was, I'd rather hear it from Ana. I stayed in my room most of the day, telling Ma I didn't feel well. The weather was humid hot—stifling, which meant wind and rain was on the way. My mind wandered . . . what would happen to our bike rides to Ana's once the weather changed? Then again, hadn't the weather already changed? My life this year was a series of storms broken only by intermittent periods of sunshine.

I spent the day thinking, writing, reflecting. I even tried meditation of the Buddhist tradition, and took a stab at Clare and Ana's style of prayer—anything to clear my mind and feel calm. I retrieved the few treasured photos of my dad and mom together. I wanted to remember him.

"What did you do?" I asked him. "Was it worth it?"

On Thursday, Rose again failed to show. It was unnerving but at least I could find out in private what happened to my dad. Clare I would have wanted by my side. Rose was still too new.

The thunderstorm had rolled in late Wednesday, leaving everything wet and refreshed. I decided to head to Ana's early. I was betting she'd be home even if it wasn't my usual time for visiting.

My risk paid off. Ana was there and didn't seem surprised at my early arrival.

"Good morning, Lily. I missed you yesterday. Have you heard from Rose?"

"No," I answered. "She didn't come over yesterday. I'm a little worried about her. Maybe her mom's sick or something."

"Yes," Ana agreed, nodding. "'Tis concerning."

"Ana, I'm sorry about last time. I was so overwhelmed by what you were telling me. You gotta understand, my mom never told me anything about my dad. I don't even know how he"—I swallowed; it was so hard to say—"how he died."

Ana was listening and nodding understandingly. She stopped suddenly, the lines on her face rearranging themselves.

"Dear child, your father isn't dead."

The light through the windows swirled briefly and dimmed. I heard a gasp, a cry. Nothing.

I woke up with a warm hand holding mine.

"Lily?" She must have felt my slight movement.

I opened my eyes. I was still on Ana's couch—slouched in a seated position.

"What happened?"

"You blacked out," Ana said.

"How long?"

"A few moments. Here, drink this." She pushed some cold tea toward me. "I'm worried about you, dear. I won't let you ride back unless I know you're okay. I can drive you. Or maybe . . . " She stopped.

"Maybe?"

"Maybe I should call your mom."

My mom. It came back to me now, why I was here, slumped on this couch, the look of concern on Ana's face. The reason I blacked out. I pulled myself up and sipped the soothing liquid.

"No," I said. "I'm okay. Don't call my mom."

"You thought your father was dead?" Ana asked.

I nodded, nursing the glass in my hands, something to clasp onto as the rest of my life fell away. When I found my voice, it was a whisper.

"All Ma ever said was, 'He is no longer with us. Do not speak it again.' I thought she meant he had died. I thought it hurt her too much to talk about." I laughed a small, bitter laugh. "Guess I was wrong."

Yeah, I guess I was wrong. Wrong about my father, wrong about my mother. My whole life Ma had let me believe my dad was dead. The sense of betrayal I felt was palpable. I wondered how I would ever trust her again. Anger and grief wrestled within me—an indescribable feeling of loss at the years I'd missed knowing my dad. But there was the other side too—the wonder of the resurrection of the dead, knowing a different future had opened up in front of me. I had a father. I would know him.

And maybe I would forgive Ma someday. But not yet.

Ana watched me carefully as the news of my dad being alive soaked in. At last she spoke. "Lily, I'm sorry you didn't know the truth about your father. I guess, under the circumstances, I understand why your mother let you believe he had passed away. Your mother lost a lot and couldn't bear losing more. The way she's lived over the years has been to protect you. It's all been for you. Remember that. Please."

I wasn't ready to think about it yet. "Ana, if you

don't mind, can you pick up the story where you left off? Tell me what happened, where my father is."

"Of course." Ana squinted her eyes as if searching her brain. "How far had I gotten?"

"You said that after the government took over food production my father unified protesters by writing an underground newspaper."

"Yes. That's right, the *Keeper*. It was working well. People across the nation were saving and secretly exchanging seeds. More and more folks were starting to plant edible landscaping, including me. Your father penned columns encouraging those who still had gardening skills to teach the younger generations. He published *how to* columns. James was instrumental in establishing and connecting groups across the country. We called them "pods," our little seed pods. Most of us felt we would have the support for political change in just a few years."

"What happened?" Now that I knew my father was alive I wasn't afraid to ask.

"What happened was Trinia Nelson. James, your father, was working hard—too hard I always thought. Someone in our group met this young woman, Trinia— short, blonde, perky type—and thought she was a good candidate for the Movement. She wasn't from around here so James was hesitant at first. She stayed around, kept complaining about the government polices, showed an interest in the old ways of food production. Eventually

James told her about Seed Savers and invited her into the group. Trinia caught on quickly and was extremely dedicated and eager. Her enthusiasm didn't end with the Movement, though. She was equally attentive to your father in a more personal way."

"Like, they were dating?" I asked.

"Your father and your mother were already an item."

"My mom?"

"You seem surprised. Your mom didn't get any recognition as a leader in the Movement, but in truth, she was one of our best teachers. In Japan, people were still allowed to grow food and your mom was from the country. She knew the old skills. Your mom taught your dad and others many things. It was she who wrote the *how to* columns published in the *Keeper*."

It was too unbelievable. Ma? The same woman who told me there were no such people as gardeners anymore?

"Ana?"

"Yes?"

"This story you're telling me—were you there? Were you a part of this group?"

"Yes."

"So you actually *knew* my dad? And you know my mom?"

She nodded. "I do."

Ana and my mom already knew each other? My mom a Seed Saver and a gardener? I shook my head. Nothing made sense.

"Shall I continue?" Ana asked.

"Uh, yeah, of course." She might as well. It couldn't get any stranger.

"As I was saying, Nelson was determined to win your father away from your mother."

I was already disliking this phantom from the past: Trinia Nelson.

"But try as she might, she was unsuccessful. When her attempts at seducing him failed, Trinia tried harder to climb the leadership ladder. It was obvious she was attempting to place herself in a position of power. Most of us thought she was simply ambitious. Looking back, it's clear she was trying to collect enough information to deal a death blow to the Movement, squashing us forever."

"She was a spy?"

Ana nodded. "An interesting thing about Ms. Nelson was that she was an absolute technology whiz. And though illegal, difficult, and highly dangerous, she wanted your father to take his underground newspaper and all of the Network online. She convinced him she could hack into the Monitor without getting caught. She told him it would be like in the old days—people everywhere would be able to connect via the Monitor and a worldwide revolution would happen. She flattered him about the power of his writing and told him to trust her."

"And Dad believed her?"

"He took it to a small group of us. James didn't want to be responsible for the decision. By that time he and your mom were married. Trinia presented her plan to us. Her blue eyes sparkled as she quoted 'research' supporting her plan and again praising James's writing skills, tossing out platitudes like confetti: *words are potent weapons, words are the most powerful thing in the universe, words are the tools, the nails*, etc. She used her technological prowess to impress us with her presentation."

Ana took my hands in hers. "Only one person remained unconvinced: your mother. It wasn't Junko's personality to be direct or confrontational, however. Mostly she questioned two things: one, the danger in putting so much information online, and two, the need. Your mom pointed out that the Movement was already doing well and such a move was unneeded. I remember the humble yet strong way your mother voiced her concerns. She was intensely serious. But she came across as cold, negative."

Ana shook her head, pursed her lips tightly for a moment.

"That's not what it was. It was the knowledge that the hard work our group had done would be wasted, flushed down the toilet if we listened to Trinia. Lives would be sacrificed and ruined and the Movement would be set back. Your mom discerned this. She also understood Trinia's persuasive power. The normally beautiful and serene Junko was not seen that night. In her place was a woman barely recognizable, burdened with the future she glimpsed on the horizon. I'm not sure if your mom suspected Trinia was an agent or if she simply intuited the dangers of the plan. Trinia, of course, tossed back her head and laughed after your mom finished speaking.

"'Oh, Junko,' I can hear those words even now, 'your hormones are out of whack with the pregnancy; don't be such a negative Nancy. You should be James's biggest cheerleader.' She actually used those words, *biggest cheerleader.* Even then I felt like gagging, the way she demeaned your mother. She walked over and put her hands on James's shoulders as she said it. It was awful. Your mom got up and walked out."

Ana stopped, as if it were the end of the story.

"My mom was pregnant with me?"

"Yes, sweetheart."

"So, so what happened?"

"Well, after your mom left, Trinia urged us to vote. Her powerful presentation and trivialization of your mother's concerns worked, a majority voted to go online. It was a setup from the beginning.

"Trinia made sure names and other identifiers of Seed Savers were part of the upload. What she said would happen, happened. For about nine hours the Network was open and ubiquitous on the Monitor. Seed Savers around the world were urged to "sign in"—long enough for those in countries such as ours to be rounded up and jailed or fined, all of their books, seeds, and plants destroyed. By the time we realized what was happening it was too late, the damage was done. Trinia was long gone before we understood we'd been tricked, that it was all a trap. Your dad had the most charges against him. He was considered a leader at the national level and an insurgent against the government. He was sentenced to forty-five years in prison. They wanted to indict Junko as well, but she pleaded for leniency on account of the pregnancy. She promised the judge she would never break the law again. Your dad was incarcerated five days after you were born."

Too much. Too much. My dad. My mom. Ana. The Movement. Trinia Nelson. Clare and Dante. Rose. Arturo. The past. The present. The future.

"Lily, are you okay?"

"I . . . I . . . It's so much. How can I face my mom? Were you close? Why didn't you mention any of this before? Where is my dad?" The questions flowed from me like a burst dam.

"None of us know for sure, but we think your father is being held at a facility in Cuba."

"Does my mom know?"

"I don't know. As far as I know, they've never communicated. Nor have your mom and I talked. It's like we're strangers. Junko fulfilled her agreement with the government. She's been a model citizen. In fact, after the crackdown GRIM agents only stayed around here for about sixteen months. We were hit so hard and so decisively in this region—broken and demoralized— that it's taken longer here to rebound than other places. We weren't even enough of a threat to be watched. At least that's what I thought until this spring. Now you understand why I stopped mentoring you children once I encountered the GRIM agent outside the church."

"And now?"

"I've been pondering that, Lily. Why, for example, the agents seem to have left? Why they were more concerned with Clare than with you? Surely they realize you are James's daughter. Has anyone visited your apartment?"

"Not that I know of . . ."

Ana shook her head slowly. "Perhaps they're convinced your mother would never risk losing you by becoming a Seed Saver again. But they suspected you children were gardening and rightly guessed an adult had to be working with you. Celia was an obvious suspect." Ana locked her eyes on me. "Then again, maybe they haven't left town."

I felt the joy of the past few weeks slipping away like water down a drain. A new distrust that made the earlier GRIM-ditching days with Clare and Dante feel like child's play was clouding over my summer.

"Lily, you and Rose shouldn't ride out here anymore. I'm sorry. I've been wanting to tell you, but couldn't think how."

I thought of my plants all over town. Then Rose. Arturo. The flagrant and thoughtless way I had been carrying on. I didn't know. I didn't know.

"I understand," I said.

16

INDECISION

Ironically, the spot I found the most solace—with my plants—was questionable in terms of safety given what I now knew. A part of me, though, the really wild in-your-face part, urged me out anyway.

As I rode through town, the wheels in my head spun in sync with the wheels of my bike. Three days ago I was feeling good about my life. I had a new friend, I was learning to cook, I had beans ripe for harvest. Now I didn't feel safe leaving the apartment. I was second-guessing everything: What had I gotten Rose into? My mom? Maybe I was even putting my father in danger.

My father, James Gardener. He's alive! He's been alive all of this time. And he's a *Seed Saver*. A writer. I smiled in spite of myself. I was like my dad.

I began at the far end of the park and walked slowly down the sidewalk, peering cautiously around. I took breaks on the benches and then sat lazily on a lone swing. I found myself replaying Ana's story from yesterday over and over in my mind. A slight breeze brought out goosebumps on my bare arms. The day was cool, a reminder that summer was almost gone. My heart ached for Clare and Dante.

"There you are!" The familiar voice cut into my mental meanderings. "What's up with ditching me?"

"What? You're the one that hasn't been showing up."

"I came by your apartment yesterday, *and today*, and you were already gone," Rose said. "I was *here* yesterday and didn't see you anywhere. By the way, I caught that *Artero* stealing your beans back at the lot."

"Rose."

"Really! I'm not lying. Check it out for yourself."

I abandoned the swing, and Rose and I rode to the lot. Sure enough, only small, spindly pods dangled from the plants.

"Told ya. When I confronted him he said you hadn't been around and that the beans would be too big. He said he was picking them for you."

Although initially upset, I thought back to a couple days ago. I remembered how fast the beans had been growing, and how big they already were. I thought about Arturo. I trusted him. Or at least I had. I wanted to. After Ana's story I didn't know if I could trust anybody. A part of me even blamed Ana for not telling the whole story to Clare, Dante, and me from the beginning. And my mom—obviously I couldn't trust her.

"They needed picking," I said. "They needed picking on Tuesday. And after the rain, I'm sure they were already too big by yesterday."

"That's what *he* said." She sounded disappointed. "Have you been hanging out with him?" Rose asked accusatorially, eyes narrowed.

"No, of course not. I did run into him one day . . . hey . . . where have *you* been?"

"Grounded."

"What?"

"I was grounded," Rose said, kicking the dirt with the toe of her sneaker. "What's the matter, Lily, never been grounded? Too goody-goody for that?"

I was not enjoying Rose's hostility. Things were confusing enough without her jabs. Actually, my mom *did not* ground; it was not in her parenting repertoire.

"Of course I've been grounded," I lied, trying to avoid more teasing. "I was just surprised. I missed you, Rose. And I was worried. You didn't show up for three days." This seemed to pacify her.

"Two days," Rose said, all spite gone from her voice. "Remember, I *did* come by yesterday. Your mom said you had already gone. She looked surprised to see me."

Shoot. Rose came by and knocked at the door? Ma knew I was gone for over an hour and not with Rose? And she never let on.

"You came to the door? I told you not to do that."

"I didn't see you, and after missing two days, I thought—"

"You thought nothing. I told you to always ride around in the parking lot." It was my turn to be irritable. "Geez, Rose, you could have gotten me in big trouble. My mom likes to know what I'm doing, who I'm with. She doesn't know about Ana."

I turned and walked back to the bikes. Rose chased after me.

"I'm sorry, Lily. I missed you, too. Now everything's straightened out. We're together. Let's go back to your place. We can pretend I caught up with you yesterday and hung out, if it helps. Then your mom won't be mad."

Everything is definitely not straightened out, I thought to myself. "That's a good idea, but I'd like to finish checking my plants. I've been neglecting them lately." I was happy to see Rose, but I wasn't finished sorting things out; my internal conversation begged to continue. Then again, maybe distraction was a good thing. I let Rose join me.

Back at the park we started at the opposite end as before. More sensitive now to the danger, I reined Rose in, reminding her of our illegal status. I commented on how good everything looked.

"I checked it all yesterday," Rose said proudly.

"And me too," a deep voice from behind added.

"Arturo," I said, turning and smiling.

"Hello. Lily, Rose," he said politely.

Rose grunted her greeting.

"How are you, Lily? I no—I *do not* see you for some time."

"Yeah, I wasn't feeling well one day . . . and then I had things to do . . . "

"I hope is okay I pick your beans. I save them for a day, but then my papa say we should eat them. There will be more fresh, later."

At this, Rose's face grew dark. Fearing oncoming rudeness, I placed my hand on her shoulder and responded quickly.

"No, of course. In fact, one reason I hadn't picked them sooner was I didn't know what to do with them. It's a secret from my mom. I'm still trying to figure out how to handle the situation."

"So, you and Rose are sneaky gardening around the city, but you don' eat the food?" His brow furrowed in perplexion.

It sounded so ridiculous when he put it that way.

"Um, things just sort of happened. And some things have changed."

Arturo nodded, as if what I said made any sense at

all. We walked as we talked, eyeing the crops, some-times chewing a little mint or basil.

"You girls gonna come see *mi jardin* soon?" Arturo asked after a while.

"Where do you live?" Rose asked.

"I will bring you there." He stared straight at me as he spoke. Fortunately, Rose was looking the other way and didn't notice.

"Maybe another time," I said. "Not today. Is it far?"

"No, no so far," Arturo said. "Very near." He raised his eyebrows lightly as he spoke.

"Great!" I said. We had circled back to the play-ground. "Well, that's it. I've already checked on the rest. I need to get going, you two."

"What do you mean, *you two?*" Rose asked.

"I have things to do at home."

"We're not going to Ana's?"

"Not today. I saw her yesterday. Today's not good for her."

"Oh."

Rose was clearly disappointed, and I felt a little guilty, but there was no way I was ready to reveal what I'd just learned about my parents. And my attempt to find solace alone with my vegetables had failed. My plan now was to do the only other thing I knew: go back home, close the door, and write.

I ran to my bicycle thinking Rose was on my heels, but when I stopped I was surprised to find myself alone.

Looking back across the park I spied Arturo crossing a street, heading toward downtown. Rose wasn't far from where I'd left her. She was talking on a telecommunicator. *That's weird*; I'd never seen her with one before. We'd never talked about it or exchanged numbers. I made a mental note to ask about it next time. Now that our daily routine was up in the air, other ways of communicating would come in handy.

I ate lunch with Ma as usual. We sat with our secrets like dead men. So this was the inheritance from my mom—the ability to pretend things were one way, when in fact they were quite the opposite.

In my room, I took out my journal and for a while simply looked at it. Today I would transcribe the story as told me by Ana. Today my journal would learn that James Gardener was alive. That he was betrayed by someone he trusted, someone who had become a friend and partner in the Movement.

I cried as I wrote, the blue lines in my notebook becoming fuzzy and thick, the teardrops scarring the paper as Ana's words had scarred my heart. I flew through the pages, writing furiously. The handwriting was large and messy at times and small and insignificant at others—the size and style mirroring my fluctuating emotions. When I was finished, I lay flat on my back staring up at the ceiling, wondering what to do next.

I pondered the timing of Ana's disclosure: Was it because I had pushed her about contacting Clare and Dante? Wouldn't it have been better to know all this before bringing in Rose? I had pushed that, too.

Lily, I said to myself, always practical, *what's done is done. Don't think about what cannot be changed. What to do now? What would Clare do?*

I figured Clare would pray. Some magical verse from the Bible would pop into her head and comfort her. I knew my friend well and this was how she operated. I didn't always understand it, but it's who she was and I respected her.

I picked up my journal. I would try it—sort of. I would attempt to write a prayer. I closed my eyes, striving to remember how I'd heard people pray. I opened my eyes and began writing:

Dear God, I don't know what to do. As you know, (wasn't God supposed to know everything?) my best friends Clare and Dante ran away because they didn't want to get caught by GRIM—and to protect their mom—and because they thought Ana was in trouble. I just found out I'm actually involved more than I thought. My parents were Seed Savers. And the danger is real. And now I have involved Rose. And then there is this guy Arturo—he knows about our gardening. Which Ana doesn't know. I never got to tell her about Arturo and now I'm not supposed to go to her house anymore and I still have too many questions. And now I feel totally weird about my mom. (I was rambling; I hoped God didn't mind ramblers)

Ana said I shouldn't visit her anymore. What do I tell Rose about that? What do I do about Arturo? Should I abandon my plants? God, I don't know what to do. And God, take care of my Dad. (It was the first time I got to talk about my dad like that. It felt good, warm.)

Amen.

I closed the journal. I would proofread later.

Immediately an idea came to me. I don't know if it was from God or just because of writing. Today was Friday. On Sunday I would go to Clare's church; maybe Ana would be there. In the meantime, I'd decide the questions I wanted to ask her.

17

ARTURO'S YARD

On Saturday Rose arrived earlier than usual. For some reason I wasn't expecting her.

After I had yelled at her, she didn't dare knock on my door. It took a moment before I recognized the loud, singing voice and looked out the window to see Rose riding circles in our parking lot, making a racket. Other apartment dwellers were starting to yell at her to shut up. I rushed down the stairs.

"Rose, quiet! Come on up," I called as gently as I could, trying to hide my face from the other tenants but knowing it was too late.

Once in my room, Rose apparently noticed I wasn't dressed for going out. "Aren't we doing our rounds this morning?" she asked.

"I'll do it this afternoon," I said. "We checked them well yesterday and this late in the year they don't need as much tending."

"What about Ana?"

"Didn't I tell you? She's not home this weekend."

"No, you didn't. You just said yesterday wasn't good."

"Oh, I'm sorry. Ana's busy all weekend. I can't hang out tomorrow either, just so you know. We should exchange numbers to save ourselves some trouble, don't you think? I didn't realize you had a telecom before—"

"What makes you think I do?" she interrupted rather rudely.

"I saw you in the park talking on one when I rode away." For a minute I thought she was going to deny it.

"Oh, yeah. My parents are making me carry one now, since the grounding."

"You never told me what you did," I said.

"I don't want to talk about it."

"Okay . . . so how about exchanging numbers? That way you don't have to knock on my door and make my mother wonder what I'm up to or make all the neighbors hate us," I said smiling, trying to lighten the conversation.

Rose hesitated. "Let me get back to you. I need to check with my folks. They might not be cool with that. This is, like, their hook in me. Not my unit for keeping up with friends."

"Oh, okay."

"I'll see you on Monday?" she asked, heading toward the door.

"Wait." I hopped off my bed and followed her. "You don't have to run off."

"That's okay. Might as well get on my parents' good side by sticking around home and helping out."

With that, Rose said goodbye to my mother and walked out.

I took my time leaving for my afternoon plant visitation, choosing to stay around home and help Ma with chores. She was very appreciative. It seemed like her origami business was constantly growing, and I couldn't help enough with the paper folding. In my mind I kept imagining a scenario where I asked her something about my dad, but I couldn't quite gather the courage.

Sometimes I felt really angry with her and other times really close. Like we were in this thing together, you know. But every time I considered how great it was that Ma knew how to garden, the conversation about gardeners flooded back into my head. No, things between my mom and me were embedded in stone. Like a granite Buddha, there would be no change.

A slight breeze whispered through the trees. I drew a deep breath and let it out slowly. Despite the weirdness in my life and the uncertainty of how to proceed with my new knowledge, for some inexplicable reason I found myself hoping to run into Arturo, wanting badly to see him. Already I'd walked the length of the park making eye contact with my lovely plant children and dawdling at the swings, people-watching, until I felt guilty for taking up space. Now, as I circled the fountain, I had given up.

"Where are you, Arturo?" I murmured as I headed to my bike near the maples.

And there he was. I swear he stepped right out from behind a tree, on cue, and was looking straight at me.

"Whu—?" My mouth fell open stupidly, and then I smiled without thinking. Instinctively, I wrested my face back under control. Too late, he had seen the grin and was smiling back and waving.

"Lily!" he called, as he jogged toward me. "Hey there, girl."

"Arturo, hi, how are you?" I may not be the well-intentioned-Asian-polite of my mom, but really, sometimes those good manners surfaced beyond my control. If I were drowning, going under, with other people nearby, my automatic polite response system would kick in. I know this because I felt like I was drowning now, and yet here I was saying "Hi, how are you?" like out of a textbook.

"I am so happy to see you today, Lily." Arturo looked around. "Where is Rose?"

"She had things to do."

"You are not afraid to come alone?" he asked.

"No. I don't mind at all. I used to come here by myself before I knew Rose."

"You don' know Rose for a long time?" He crinkled his brow.

"No. We've only been hanging out for a few weeks." We had reached my bike.

"You are leaving? Lily, you can come to my house now?"

His eyes pleaded with me. I knew I shouldn't. What did I really know about Arturo? Yet something about the despondency of my situation urged me to throw caution to the wind. I would not be my mother. I refused to bow to my fears in exchange for life in a box while others were on the outside, defying the rules.

"Yes, Arturo. Now is a really good time for me to visit your home."

He smiled his biggest smile, the one showing off his perfect white teeth.

"Is not far, follow me," he said as he ran away.

I climbed on my bicycle and rode, easily catching up. I laughed as I pedaled alongside the running young man. "What, you gonna run all the way home?"

"Why not?" he asked. "Afraid you cannot to keep up?"

Arturo jogged effortlessly through the old part of downtown. Eventually I hopped off and walked my bike after nearly hitting a woman pushing a stroller.

When Arturo noticed I wasn't beside him, he dashed back and walked with me.

"I thought you said it was very near?"

"*Sí*. Almost there."

I rolled my eyes, causing him to laugh.

Now through downtown and just out the other side, I noticed pocket neighborhoods of small older homes down short, narrow roads; whole residential sections I'd never before noticed.

"There," Arturo said, nodding toward the next lane. "Turn there."

We turned down a road stippled with potholes and absent of sidewalks. At the very end of the street—it was a dead-end—Arturo stopped in front of a tiny white house with peeling paint.

"Here," he announced. "*Mi* castle . . . get it," he urged, "*mi casa, mi castle?*"

I smiled weakly at his joke, suddenly feeling insecure. What was I doing? I looked behind me and all around, studying my surroundings.

Arturo missed nothing. "'S okay, Lily," he said, his hand on my shoulder. "No one follow you. Always, I am watching."

His statement startled me. *Always, I am watching?*

"Please, come in." He opened the door and took ahold my bike, pulling it inside behind me.

The room was cramped and dark, illuminated only by its small windows.

"Excuse," Arturo said, "we save electricity for other."
He called out ahead of us. "*Abuelo!* Lily is here."

We walked straight through the house and out the
back. An old man was rocking in a wicker chair under
a hastily-made awning. He wore a straw hat and held
a pint-sized dog. The man turned and watched as we
came through the door.

"*Buenas tardes,*" he said, nodding.

"Papa is still at work—"

Arturo stopped midsentence as he turned and saw
my face. My eyes had wandered from the old man to
the yard. I had expected something different. The way
Arturo talked about his garden I'd imagined something
. . . well . . . something beautiful. Instead, the yard
resembled an abandoned lot filled with weeds and junk.
My normal poker face failed to hide the disappointment. Arturo's eyes, too, betrayed him—registering his
own disappointment in me.

"Come, Lily, look. Look close." Arturo grabbed my
hand and pulled me after him, off the concrete slab and
out into the yard. "You see?" he urged.

I saw weeds. I kept looking.

"Here," Arturo said, breaking off a flowering plant
and putting it first under his nose and then under mine.
"You know it?"

It was familiar, one of the herbs I'd grown, but
which one?

"Cilantro," he said.

"It flowers?"

"Yes, of course. It make seed for us to save and plant more."

I looked around, trying to spot familiar plants.

"Most of these are weeds, aren't they?" I asked.

"¡Ay! What is a weed? A weed is only a plant that is unwanted where it grow." Arturo pointed to the multitude of blooming dandelions in the yard. "People eat these for hundreds of years. Is good."

I stood and stared. Could this be true? People ate weeds?

"You don' believe me? Here," he plucked a flower, then a leaf. "Taste."

I took a nibble. "Bleh." Not good.

Arturo laughed. "Sorry. Is no so good, now. Better before the flower starting. But I like. And is good later, after the cold *tambien*."

Arturo moved through the tangled yard like a ship in familiar harbor, pointing out vegetables I hadn't noticed and weeds he said were edible. In the stacks of tires and old sinks, vegetation of all sorts spilled out. Arturo raised his eyebrows, nodding toward an unfamiliar and luscious green plant.

"Potatoes."

I remembered potatoes. I had read about them but hadn't planted any. I had no 'seed potatoes' to get started. From what I recalled, potatoes had been an important staple in countries around the world and were still grown here and used in our processed food groups. They were an underground crop. Arturo definitely had my attention now and he knew it.

"How . . . " I didn't know what I wanted to ask.

"You want to see?"

I nodded.

Crouching down, Arturo put his fingers around the base of the plant, feeling in the dirt. "Ah," he said, "a nice one. *Abuelo*," he shouted back at his grandfather, something in Spanish. The old man laughed.

"Good one," he told me, "big. I am surprising *Abuelo* miss. He like to steal some new potatoes during the summer."

Arturo grabbed my hand, pulling me down, then placed it in the dirt onto a firm round potato, its red skin slightly showing aboveground. "Potato," he said, close to my ear. "*Papa* in Spanish." The whisper in my ear sent goosebumps scurrying across my shoulder blades and down my arms. Our hands were together in a treasure chest of gold. My heart beat fast and I felt warm all over. I wasn't sure at which moment my excitement over the potato changed into an awkwardness at my nearness to Arturo, even though his hand no longer covered mine but was off searching for more potatoes. He was pulling them out of the ground, dusting them off.

"Go on, Lily, try to find."

I gathered myself together, concentrating on the

garden rather than my emotions. I dug around, but all I felt was dirt.

"Try another," he said, pointing toward other potato plants I now recognized growing in old barrels and appliances.

"How?" I faltered, finding my voice at last.

"Like I show you. Feel near the plant, how you say, soft."

"Gently?"

"Yes," he smiled, "gently."

My fingers poked down at the base of the next plant. I didn't mind the dirt pressing under my nails. I moved my hand out away from the base and hit something hard. I felt out the shape of it. "I found one!" I called. I remembered the time Dante pulled the first carrot from the ground. More buried treasure.

"Big?" Arturo asked.

I pulled my hand out and showed him the size with my fingers.

"Okay," he answered. "Take it out, Lily."

Carefully I pulled the tennis ball sized potato out of the ground, satisfaction flooding my soul.

Time melted away in the summer heat as Arturo patiently and proudly showed me everything growing in his back yard. As I sat, later, sipping tea with him and his grandfather, I was amazed at how my view of his yard had changed over the course of the afternoon.

What had initially looked to me like a trashed-out vacant lot, now seemed a lush and verdant garden filled with life and promise.

"In California," Arturo said now, "is different. Many people grow. Here, here is like a cloud cover everything. My papa say there must be a reason. He no—he *do not* want to stop growing, but he is afraid, a little. Something in this town . . . " Arturo shook his head as he trailed off.

"Arturo, your father is right."

Maybe I shouldn't have, but I told Arturo everything. The history of Seed Savers and GRIM and the role our town had played in it. I kept secret the part about my dad and mom, but I did tell him about Clare and Dante and me—without divulging Ana's identity. When I finished, Arturo let out a long, slow whistle.

"Oh," he said, "this explains it."

"Yeah. Well it's good to know every place isn't as bad as here," I said.

"Yes," he agreed. "Hey, Lily, I enjoy talking with you. I want to talk more, but I think maybe is time for you to go?"

Time? The time! I had completely lost track of the time—my eyes searched for a clock. "What time is it?"

"Is six o'clock."

"Six o'clock! Oh, no. My mom will kill me!" I got up and ran through the house, pulling my bike to the street. Arturo trailed after me.

"I will accompany you," he called.

"It's okay," I yelled back, already pedaling. "Thanks, see you later." I glanced back a couple of times. Arturo ran several blocks before falling back in exhaustion.

18

SUSPICIONS

I'm not proud to say it, but I lied to Ma that night. I told her I'd been at Rose's house and we had gotten carried away playing an old-fashioned board game, forgetting the time. I sat sullen-faced through her scolding and spent the remainder of the evening in my room.

I couldn't stop thinking about Arturo. I tried to plan what to say to Ana the next day at church, should I find her, but I couldn't focus. Over and over I was at Arturo's house, under the awning, his hand grabbing mine, pulling me along. Or down in the dirt, his hand guiding mine in search of potatoes.

I wanted to write about these feelings but didn't dare. It embarrassed me. I'd never been the kind of girl who clamored for boys' attention. I recalled how in fifth grade some of the girls started talking about "hot" guys. Bleh. Clare and I thought it was dumb. Not that we didn't have friends who were guys. Well, collectively, anyway. Like I said before, Clare was more handy with the male population. But this wasn't like with Henry or LaMonte. This, for all apparent purposes, was a crush. Me, Lily Gardener, experiencing my first crush.

It took a long time to fall asleep, but eventually ideas about what to discuss with Ana had emptied from my head into my notebook, freeing me to drift off. In the morning I awoke early, nervous about the task at hand but refreshed and ready. My new feelings for Arturo gave me a buoyancy and energy to tackle the day.

I decided to tell Ma the truth—that I planned to attend church at St. Vincent's. I'd ridden by to check the time of the service and discovered there were two services. Not knowing which one Ana attended, I figured I'd visit both.

"Why you want to go to church?" Ma asked.

"I miss Clare and Dante," I answered. This was not a lie. "It's their church."

I knew which buttons to push with Ma. She nodded her head in understanding, her eyes moistening.

"Okay," she said. "Good."

"Um," I added, "I'm not sure when I'll be back. Church people sometimes eat together afterwards." This, of course, I totally made up based on a novel I read.

She eyed me, not suspiciously really, more like concern.

"Lily, don't be gone all day. Maybe you take the telecom and call me if you will be very late?"

"Okay, sure, Ma." I hated using the telecom, but maybe it was a good idea. Somewhere in the back of my head I entertained the notion of seeing Arturo again.

I wasn't sure how to dress for church, so decided to go with my nicest clothes—which isn't saying a lot. I rode the short distance and parked my bike with the others.

Although intending to be early, I was surprised at the number of people already inside. A long center aisle and two side aisles led up to a stage behind which hung a statue of a man on a cross. What was it Christians believed? It was foggy to me. I'd heard the story, but it all jumbled together in my brain—baby Jesus born in a stable . . . a cross . . . heaven and hell. *Some other time, Lily*, I told myself. *Focus*. Just then she turned—Ana! She was inside the large room, midway up, seated on one of the long wooden benches. Having seen me, she turned again and waved me in. I hurried down the aisle and slid in next to her.

"Ana," I whispered.

"Shh, not now," she said, finger to her lips. "Later." She nodded her head forward and sat in silence.

It was my first ever church service. I liked some parts but grew bored during others. I felt out of place, not knowing when to stand, sit, kneel. The words to say when everyone spoke together. But I did feel close to Clare and Dante. The service helped me glimpse the friends I dearly missed.

Finally it ended. I followed Ana out to what she called "the foyer."

"Lily," she said. "How nice to see you. Is everything okay?"

"I need to talk to you, Ana. I have some questions."

She glanced around. "Let me see if I can find a room where we can talk. Come along." Ana spoke with a man, and in a few moments we walked down a hall and into a small classroom.

"Okay, Lily. Go ahead."

"Well, um . . . " it was hard to know where to begin. I looked at my hand where I'd jotted notes, the ink smeared and ugly. "If I'm not allowed to visit you anymore, what should I tell Rose? She'll be expecting to ride out there."

"Yes, I've thought about that. School will be starting soon. Until then, perhaps you can convince her to ride in another direction? Or maybe for this week, tell her I've gone to visit relatives—though I'd prefer we not tell tales. I'm sorry. I regret having let it go this far."

"Is it okay to meet you here if I need to?"

"Yes. This is a fine place to meet. But as always, be discreet."

I thought about the vegetable plants I had kept

secret from Ana, not so discreet—but I held my silence.

"Anything else?" Ana asked, eyebrows lifting.

I opened my mouth to speak, then closed it, looking down at my hands. Arturo, too, would remain my secret. What possible good would come from Ana knowing I'd told another person about our dubious activities?

"Yes?" She waited.

I looked up at her. "Are you sure you won't teach me how to communicate directly with the Network?"

Ana sighed. "No, Lily. I've already gotten you kids into too much trouble. I will not jeopardize you further. Please don't worry needlessly about things that may or may not happen in some unknown future."

"Then what should I worry about?" I'd said it out loud before I could stop myself.

Ana gave me one of those wise but gentle looks of hers. "My dear, I've found that in most instances hope and faith work better than worry and fear."

I didn't know how to respond, but what she said reminded me of Clare. It was no wonder the two of them had found each other. Sometimes they seemed to be the older/younger versions of themselves.

After that Ana and I chatted a little more, talked about the good times, imagined what Clare and Dante were up to, then hugged and said goodbye. Though cautioning me strongly to be careful, Ana urged me not to give up my studies of gardening. In a low voice she told me that though it might not seem like it, nationwide the

Movement was gaining strength. There was dissension in the government concerning the current food policy and funding for GRIM was on the line. Increasing numbers of dissidents like us were banding together. I left St. Vincent's feeling hopeful.

Before heading home, I decided to peruse my lots and waysides, and of course, the park. I wasn't surprised when I felt a tap on my shoulder.

"Hi, Lily."

"Hi, Arturo."

"I see you in church today."

"Whu—?"

"I see you leaving first service. You walking down a hall with your *abuela*."

"My what?"

"Your grandmother. I call to you, but you don' hear me."

"You go to St. Vincent's?" I asked.

"Sure. But I never see you there before. I should change to first service," Arturo said, smiling.

"No, I—"

"No?" he pouted. "You don' want me in your service?"

"Arturo," I punched his arm playfully, "I don't attend St. Vincent's . . . I needed to see the woman you saw me with—she's not my grandmother."

He raised his eyebrows, waiting for me to continue. I didn't feel like explaining.

"Hey, how'd you get here so fast if you were at second service?" I asked.

"The service end twenty minutes ago—where you been?"

True, I had checked my other plots first. "Oh," I answered dumbly, "yeah."

"Hungry, Lily? You like to come to my house for lunch?"

I checked the time on my telecom. I'd love to spend the day with Arturo.

"Sure," I said. "Let me call my mom, first."

I told Ma I was eating with a friend I ran into at church and asked if we could spend the afternoon together. Happy I had checked in, she easily gave permission. Crazy as it sounds, I found myself humming as I rode to Arturo's, the nutty kid running behind me the entire way.

Once again, we entered the small, dark living room. And once again, Arturo shouted as he entered, "*Abuelo*, Poppy, I am home. And I bring Lily."

Leaving my bike by the door, we passed through to the back room, better lit from the larger, south facing windows. Arturo's grandpa sat just outside, in the same chair as before. His father, in the tiny kitchen, stood over a contraption I did not recognize. Smoke from an open flame clouded the room, causing me to choke and cough.

"*Hola*, Lily," Arturo's father said, extending a hand, "excuse."

Arturo laughed, setting loose the butterflies in my stomach. "We like to grill meat, but we afraid the good smell maybe get us in trouble, so my dad cook inside."

"Meat?"

"You no—you *don't* know *meat?*" he asked. "*Carne?*"

"Changing into Spanish is not going to help," I reminded him.

"You know only about plants make food?"

"Yes." I was puzzled. It was coming back now. I remembered seeing the word *meat* in some of the books. But we hadn't covered it in class with Ana. She hadn't wanted to discuss it. "Meat is like Protein, right?"

"*Jess.*"

"Well?"

"Well, what?" he asked, fishy-like.

"Aren't you going to tell me more about meat?"

"More?" His eyes were wide with innocence.

Just then, Arturo's dad finished his cooking and bustled us outside to eat. I cannot tell you exactly what I ate, but I can tell you it was the best meal I'd ever tasted. We started with a flat, round Carbo-type thingy, and placed on it strips of the grilled meat. Next we added chopped onions, cilantro, green leaves, and peppers, finishing with green and red sauces. We folded the flat Carbos—I can't remember what they were called—and bit in. I felt, then, that I would spend my life fighting for food freedom if only to eat such a meal again.

Peppers, by the way, come in many varieties, as does all food, apparently. They were beautiful colors: red, green, orange, yellow. Some were sweet and others spicy hot. At first, the men wouldn't allow me to eat the peppers they were eating. They said they were too "hot" for me. I couldn't understand how something uncooked could be hot, so finally they let me try. Even *Abuelo* laughed himself into a frenzy at my resulting coughing and watery eyes. After they helped me "put out the fire," as Arturo's papa described it, we continued stuffing ourselves with the delicious food until we could eat no more, finishing with a sweet, flowery tea. Not one of them would answer my questions as to the origin of meat.

Arturo and I washed the dishes together, talking and laughing, but staying away from serious topics such as family, things legal and not legal, and emotions. Then Arturo excused himself, stepping into the yard, and spoke to his father and grandfather in Spanish. I could tell the subject matter was serious and that Arturo was meeting with resistance. At last he returned.

"I am sorry for you waiting, Lily. I want to show you something."

He led me down some stairs into a basement.

"This is why we no use lamps upstairs," Arturo told me as we walked.

Light from the basement flooded up as we descended. And then I saw it, towers and tables filled with lush green plants: tomatoes and peppers plants hanging full with large and colorful fruit; small purple bells dangling from bushy plants I didn't recognize; cucumber vines snaking around gutters filled with colorful lettuce and vibrant herbs. Around the edges of the room small fans whirred.

"Greenhouse. We save electricity from other things so no . . . mmm . . . is notice using more than normal. Is less vegetables here now," Arturo said, "because is more plants outside in summer." He smiled with pride.

To say I was stunned would be like saying the Grand Canyon was a nice little hole. "What do you do with it all?" I asked.

"Always, we eat fresh," he said. "Even in winter— some. We harvest seeds. We trade with others. Same with food. It is the business of my grandfather and I. The immigrant workers do not like your type of food."

"But, Arturo—"

"Yes, is illegal, Lily. We know. Hey, I am not the one planting herbs in the park and beans in vacant lots!"

I blushed. He was right. Who was more likely to be caught?

"Your face is change to red," Arturo observed. "Whatsamatter, you like me?" He stepped closer, taking my hands.

I pulled away.

"Sorry, Lily. I no—I *don't* want you to feel bad. Sorry."

"It's okay." I started up the stairs. "I think I should go," I said, my words trailing behind me.

"Lily, wait!" Arturo was skipping steps, trying to catch up. "I need to talk to you about something more."

I stopped, and he passed around me.

"Come outside."

Back outside, we sat on the edge of what was once a bathtub but was now a miniature garden.

"Lily," Arturo said, "you should be careful about Rose."

What? I was caught off guard. I'd been expecting something along the lines of what had just happened between us, or perhaps being sworn to secrecy about the family business.

"I don' trust her," he continued.

"What? Why not? What are you talking about?"

"You don' know her a long time, right?"

"That's right. But you and I don't—*haven't* known each other very long."

"You, uh, been to her place?" he asked, then mumbled something in Spanish.

"No."

"What you really know about Rose?" he prodded. "You know her last name?"

I didn't. I didn't even know Rose's last name. I shook my head no.

"She look at me with hate," Arturo said, lifting an eyebrow. "I no, *I don'* trust her."

"Arturo, I admit, she doesn't seem to like you. But that doesn't mean you can't trust her."

"On one day when you don' is with her, she ask to come to my house. She know me only little and she ask me to show my house. I think, uh, is suspicious."

"But you invited us both to your house! You can't hold that against her."

Arturo looked at me skeptically, disappointed perhaps, arms crossed defensively in front of himself.

"You be careful, *m'ija*."

I jumped to my feet, ignoring his last remark. "Okay, so is that it? I really should be going."

A smile melted away his sternness and once again Arturo was the sweet boy I'd so quickly grown fond of.

"Let's go," he said, his hand on my shoulder as we walked to my bike.

I arrived home around 4 p.m., still plenty of time to enjoy a lovely summer evening with Ma. All things considered, I was feeling pretty good. I invited Ma out for a walk which she gladly accepted. She asked me a few obligatory questions about my day, and I answered with the expected responses.

Then, to both her horror and mine, someone living inside my body asked, "How did you meet my dad?"

"Lily—"

"I'm sorry, Ma, I—"

"—no, do not be sorry. You are becoming a young

woman. Love will be on your mind."

Now I was really embarrassed. Was I that transparent?

She continued. "It was a different time then, Lily, a better time—and a worse time. The world changes. We go on. We adapt. I was . . . "

Ma went on talking but I missed whatever it was she said. Something about the way she spoke distracted me. Her English—it seemed more fluent than usual—was it my imagination?

" . . . and he was so good to me. So patient, so kind. He believed in me and I returned his kindness and love with my own."

She turned, a smile lighting her face as I'd rarely seen. It wasn't my imagination. There was more to my mother than I knew. Not only had she kept secrets about my father, she had hidden away herself as well. A part of me wanted to cry, but seeing her beaming face as she spoke lovingly of my father, more than anything else, made me happy.

"Thanks, Ma," I said, reaching out and squeezing her hand.

I wrote in my journal for an entire hour that night. First about Ana's advice at church, then all things Arturo, and ending with my walk with Ma.

I reflected on the fact that I would turn thirteen tomorrow—without Clare, yet with this new perplexing *guy* relationship. As much as I disliked putting my emotions and experiences about Arturo on paper, I could hold it in no longer. I only hoped no one ever set eyes inside my journal. I now understood those dumb diaries with the locks and keys. Not one question was answered by writing it all down, but I felt better having done it.

After that I practiced what I would say to Rose and wondered how she would take the news about not visiting Ana. Rose had a short attention span; maybe it wouldn't bother her at all. I would find out soon enough.

But the next day Rose *didn't* show up. Not in the morning. Not for lunch. And not in the afternoon. I stayed home all day, waiting. *Some way to spend my birthday.* I should have given her my number even if she didn't want to give me hers.

Something needled me. The questions raised by Arturo lingered. Was it so strange I didn't know Rose's last name and that I hadn't been to her apartment? Maybe not, but what *was strange* was the way she'd been acting lately. And now she had disappeared *again*.

Why had Arturo been so adamant about her? I'd written it off as a response to Rose's open hostility toward him, but was there more? Did Arturo know something he wasn't sharing?

19

RETURN OF GRIM

On Tuesday morning the telecom rang. "Lily," Ma called, "for you." I thought Rose had somehow gotten my number.

"Hello?"

"Lily, this is Father Williams, from St. Vincent's. It seems you left an item at church on Sunday."

"Really?" I couldn't think of anything. "I don't think—"

"—Lily, please come get it as soon as possible. I'm here waiting for you."

"—but—"

The telecom clicked off.

"Ma, that was the priest at the church. He said I left something and for me to come right away. I'm gonna ride over and get it. Keep an eye out for Rose, okay? I won't be long."

"Okay, Lily, be careful."

The church doors were unlocked. Father Williams met me just inside.

"Come, child," he said. He led me to the small room where Ana and I had spoken two days earlier. Ana sat waiting.

"Ana?"

"Oh, Lily! Lily, are you safe?"

"What's wrong?" She looked scared, worried.

"Lily, they came yesterday. GRIM agents. They searched my house and yard. They asked where I hid my Monitor. They yelled at me when I said I didn't own one." Her hands shook. I reached out and held them.

"They pulled out my plants—flowers, herbs, weeds—it didn't matter which. They yanked up whatever they saw. Ignorant," she spat out the word like a bitter taste in her mouth. "I had a few things on the counter, in the fridge. They charged me $700 in fines. They said they knew I was a member of Seed Savers. That they know you and Rose have been visiting me. I told them, yes, it was true, I was your tutor. They couldn't find anything to prove the Seed Savers charge. The law requires evidence linking me to Seed Savers or proof that I've taught gardening to others. Hearsay and a few odd plants on my property isn't enough."

I stared at Ana with wide eyes, not knowing what to say.

"Lily, I'm worried about you and Rose. Forgive me for summoning you here like this, but I didn't know a safe way to get in touch with you—and you needed to know. I guess all along I was the one responsible for Clare and Dante getting into trouble . . . At least you and Rose weren't at my home having a lesson. They would have caught us red-handed. And I'm glad Rose wasn't any further involved . . ."

As Ana rambled, a horrible feeling began creeping into my gut, spreading like an incoming tide. I was trying to put it all together—Rose not coming over yesterday, the same day GRIM raided Ana's home . . . For all Rose knew, I had met with Ana for more lessons . . . which meant . . .

"Ana—do you think kids can be spies?"

I told Ana my fears about Rose, Rose's recent strange behavior, and the telecom incident. Ana wasn't ready to believe Rose was one of the bad guys. For that matter, neither was I. Maybe it was a coincidence.

"Rose didn't seek you out this summer, did she?" Ana asked.

"No, she didn't." I recalled how we met at the fountain that first day. How I needed to befriend her to cover my lie.

Ana's confidence in Rose made me feel better. As

we talked on, I sensed Ana calming, gaining back her inner strength. She was rattled, yes, but not defeated. As before, Ana encouraged me to be brave but her plea for caution was stronger than ever. I knew then my vegetables were on their own.

When it was all over, we hugged. I thanked Ana for letting me know what had happened, and she thanked me for coming.

I rode home without thinking—or maybe thinking too much. When I pulled into our complex I couldn't remember having made any of the stops or turns. I had been on autopilot, thoughts swirling like a cyclone in my head as I pedaled: GRIM was still watching and I hadn't noticed. Who would be interrogated next? I worried about whether I'd placed my parents in jeopardy. And I still wondered about Rose's convenient absence the day GRIM raided Ana's house.

Imagine my shock when I walked into the apartment and found Rose seated at the table with my mother, talking about the approaching school year.

"Rose?"

"Hey, you're back," she said, turning to face me. "Where have you been? I mean, I know you had to go to the church, but you've been gone a long time."

"Uh . . . yeah." Despite Ana's trust in Rose, I advanced cautiously. There was still Arturo's strange warning to consider. "Well, I ran into somebody I knew and, you know, we talked for awhile . . . " Fortunately, she wasn't paying attention. True to form, Rose had moved on.

"Hey, sorry about yesterday. Jen and me went shopping. Dad got a work bonus and we got to go buy stuff. Wanna ride?" she asked. I thought about giving her a cold stare on account of forgetting my birthday. *Not worth it.*

"Of course," I said. *Think fast,* I told myself as we walked to the bikes. I took the lead and steered Rose in a new direction. She followed without question. We circled around and arrived back home.

"Aren't we going to Ana's today?"

"No," I said. "I've decided it's too far. The days are getting shorter, and the weather is changing. I'd feel more comfortable sticking closer to home."

"Yeah, I hear ya," Rose agreed. "I felt that way myself but didn't want to be a stick-in-the-mud."

I turned and looked straight at her. "Maybe we can go to your place sometime." She didn't flinch.

"Sure. I thought you'd never ask."

You could have knocked me over with a straw. "Oh," I replied dumbly. "Cool. Rose, what's your last name?"

"O'Connor."

She looked at me funny. "Anything else, Sherlock?" she teased.

"Um, no. I'm good. Wanna come up for a snack?"

We dropped the bikes and headed up the stairs,

my doubts about Rose as transitory as a bubble in the wind.

20

SEEDS OF DOUBT

Rose showed up precisely at nine the next morning to guide me to her apartment. It wasn't far, and I wondered why we'd never gone there before. True, it was in a slightly seedier part of the neighborhood, and my mom did keep a cleaner home. Could this have kept Rose from inviting me? Or was it because she liked getting away from her younger sister? Lisa was quite annoying.

We hung around her place awhile, then scouted our regular haunts, though we left the vegetables alone. I told her I had reason to be more cautious and she was okay with that.

Of course we ran into Arturo. Rose was cold, but decent. Arturo was pleasant as usual, which amazed me knowing how he really felt about Rose. It was a bit unnerving how well he masked his emotions.

The day was hot—sweltering to be precise. After cooling off in the fountain we hit Rose's place again for drinks. We reminisced about Ana's ice cold tea and swore someday we would own working refrigerators.

"Lily?"

"Yeah?"

"It's been fun hanging out with you."

"Yeah," I said.

"I liked learning that stuff from Ana."

"Mm-hmm."

"D'ya think she'll be working at St. Vincent's again?"

I froze. Trap question, or true interest? "I . . . uh . . . I don't know. But she won't do any more garden teaching."

"Why not?"

"Don't you remember? I told you she refused to continue tutoring after she saw the agent."

"But what about our visits to her house?"

"My mistake," I said.

"*Our* mistake," Rose corrected. "If it *was* a mistake."

I wanted to let her know what a big mistake it had been. But a tiny part of me was still not certain about Rose. Arturo had planted seeds of doubt.

"It wasn't a good idea," I said. "Just because neither of us has seen an agent since Clare and Dante left doesn't mean they're not around. I should have learned my lesson before."

"You're right," Rose said. "There is that. Their mom got arrested."

This set me back, thinking about Clare and Dante and not knowing where they were. Ana's recent disturbance fresh in my mind. I looked down, silent in my descending despair.

Rose kept talking. "Lily, I hate to say this, because I've seen the way you look at him, but I don't trust that Arturo."

I looked up. *What*?

"I know it's unlikely he's a GRIM agent, but what if, you know, what if he works for them. Like, if he was an illegal and they cut him a deal. I mean, he could have been keeping tabs on us, right? But then I spotted him, so he had to act all nice. He could be like, twenty-three years old or something. Those foreigners often look younger than their actual age."

Sometimes Rose was so clueless. She knew I was half Japanese. I stared at her, giving her my best laser death glare, but she kept right on talking.

"I'm just saying, I think if we're gonna be careful, we need to be careful all the way around."

I blinked and shook my head slightly. "What? You think Arturo might be a spy for GRIM?" I so wanted to tell her he thought the same about her.

"He could be. Think about it—he suddenly shows up watching our every move. Then when we call him on it, he's all friendly."

"He might say the same about you."

"Did he?" she asked, her voice rising.

"I said, *he might.*"

"It's not even true," she said. "First of all, we met months ago at tutoring. Second, I wasn't sneaking around watching you in the park—remember?"

She was right, of course. This conversation was going nowhere. "Yes, Rose, I remember. Look, I think we're just spooking ourselves. At this rate we won't be trusting anybody." I looked around, eyes narrowed. "Say, where is your sister?" I asked suspiciously.

We laughed, then jumped on the bikes and headed back to my place.

The next morning I was surprised to find Arturo waiting outside my apartment building.

"Arturo!"

"Lily, hi. Let's walk."

"You really need a bike," I told him.

"So I hear. Hey, why you still going with Rose?"

Wow. Sometimes his English skills made him sound too abrupt. "Umm, last time I checked, this was still a semifree country."

"Lily."

"Look, Arturo. Rose is okay. I am being careful," I stressed. "You know, Rose pointed out that maybe *you* were a spy." I laughed after I said it. It was a joke.

Arturo gazed at me stonily. "Not funny."

I didn't want to do this. I liked Arturo. Seeing this side of him was not fun. "Oh brother. Forget it, okay? I'm fine. But—" I was about to tell him of Ana's encounter, that there really were GRIM agents around. I changed my mind.

"But—?"

"But I've decided to be more careful and abandon my public gardening," I said.

"Good idea. Will you garden with the old woman of who you talk?"

"No. I mean . . . school's about to start. And it's too far to go, really."

He nodded.

"I was wondering," I continued, "about your plant lights in the basement—"

"Shh," he placed a finger to his lips.

"Where do you get those?" I whispered.

"I will tell you sometime," he said. "But . . . uh . . . not today."

"Arturo?"

"*Jess?*"

"Which school will you be attending?"

He hesitated.

"School starts soon," I continued, "which school is yours?" I wasn't sure of the boundary lines, or even which grade Arturo was in.

"I don' know," he answered. His smile was weak, forced. "I suppose I need to find out."

21

CONFESSION

Every day school drew nearer I felt more and more panicked. Like I couldn't go back—not without Clare. I clung to summer like a cat on a screen door.

"Lily," Rose said—it was our last long weekend before school—"have you talked to Ana recently?"

"Not really."

She was silent, unusual for Rose.

"Why do you ask?"

"Just wondered. Do you think she's okay?"

Alarms went off inside me. Rose had a strange look on her face, like a child who's just suffered a potty training setback.

"Rose?"

"Lily, I'm sorry."

She started crying. Crying! I had never seen Rose cry. She was a tough as nails no-nonsense kid. Before I knew it, I was across the room, shaking her.

"Why wouldn't Ana be okay?" I yelled.

"I didn't want to do it. My stepmom made me. She said we needed the money. I had no choice."

"Rose—"

"She seemed really nice. But I wasn't fooled. I stood right up to her. But Jen—"

"—Rose, start at the beginning, tell me what you're talking about—is Ana okay?" My voice rose in panic. I closed the door and turned up the music so Ma wouldn't hear.

"I don't know," Rose cried. "That's why I asked if you'd talked to her."

"I talked to Ana on Tuesday," I said. "GRIM agents visited her on Monday. What do you know?"

"She's okay?" Rose sniffed and seemed relieved.

"Why? What do you know about it?" I said again.

Rose hesitated.

"Tell me!" I screamed.

Rose shook loose from my grip and began speaking. "A while back, a woman showed up at our apartment. She told my stepmom, Jen, that I had information she'd pay us for. Jen said I'd help, without knowing what the woman wanted. I wasn't home. Later, the woman came again when I *was* home and Jen shoved me in front of her. The lady looked kinda nice—not threatening. Small, middle-aged. But her eyes were cold and her smile wasn't really there."

For the first time, Rose looked up, met my gaze.

"It was like there was a smile on the outside of her face, but it didn't go all the way through—like a mask. When she spoke, her words said one thing, but you knew they meant exactly the opposite. I don't know who she was, but I think she was GRIM. She gave us fancy new telecommunicators. She asked lots of questions. Questions about you, and Clare, and Ana, and Celia, and your mom—"

"*My mom?*"

Rose nodded. "She wanted me to keep hanging out with you. Said she'd be back."

"What did you tell her?"

Rose hung her head, unable to sustain eye contact. "Well, you saw me that day in the park with the telecom. I was reporting where you were. But Lily, I couldn't do it. Everything I did, I did and said the least I could, and I only did it because my stepmom made me. I told the lady the plants you tended around town were planted by Clare and Dante. I said I didn't know if Ana taught you guys about gardening, but that for me personally she only helped with math and English."

I listened without interrupting, barely daring to breathe.

"The lady didn't believe me, I could tell by her face.

She knew you and me had been to Ana's house and wanted to know what we did there. I admitted we'd been there and that we drank tea, but I said the tea was from plant leaves anybody could find. I lied about the books. 'Books?' I said, 'What books?' She asked me about seeds, too. Did you have any, did Ana have any. Jen glared at me, but I played dumb. *I liked* learning that stuff. I want to grow my own food and tea leaves. I didn't rat anybody out."

Rose paused. I waited.

She inhaled and let out a long sigh. "Anyway, I had to come clean with you. I couldn't live with myself anymore. And I needed to know about Ana." She stopped. At last she looked up at me, chewing her lip.

I felt dead, deflated. Like a slashed tire, flat on the ground, with the weight of the entire car bearing down on me. During Rose's confession, a variety of emotions had surged through me: fear, betrayal, anger, sadness, empathy, doubt. And now everything stopped. Like at the end of a fast-moving and terror-filled amusement ride, I sat immobile but inwardly reeling.

"Lily?" Rose's eyes asked if we were still friends.

I wanted to tell her it was okay, that I understood. But it wasn't okay and I didn't understand. I had trusted Rose. As I met Rose's penitent gaze, all I could see was Ana's shaken and fearful countenance.

"I can't, Rose, not yet." I paused. "You should leave now." I crossed the room and opened the door. She ran out of my room and through the apartment, hiding her tear-stained face from Ma.

I turned the music back down and stared up at the ceiling, trying to remember what it was like to have a boring, uneventful summer.

How could I have been so stupid? I no longer knew what to believe or whom to trust. Maybe what Rose said was true, or maybe it was just a cover. Maybe because we'd stopped visiting Ana and my plants, agent Rose had been instructed to "confess" so that I would trust her again and they could catch Ana in the act. I thought back, way back. At tutoring Rose had been nosy, watchful . . . and yet . . . I had grown to really like Rose. It felt true what she had told me. Her tears seemed like real tears.

I didn't know what to do. It was too much even for my journal. School was starting in three days. In my mind's eye, I saw a cartoon pile of dynamite, the fuse burning shorter, an explosion imminent.

22

LILY'S DECISION

I walked out of the old brick building alone, my eighth grade schedule in hand. Health? Language Arts? Chinese? I crumpled up the paper and tossed it into the nearest trash can. I would not be needing this.

At home I gathered my journals and hid them in the crawl space under the apartment building. Of Ana's books, I kept three and took the rest to St. Vincent's. I didn't dare leave them at home. For some reason I viewed the church as a kind of sanctuary. Maybe because of how Father Williams stepped in to help Ana and me. I knew the doors there were always open. I sneaked away from home, my load hidden in my backpack. In the church I found a room filled with books and slipped mine in among Self-help and Religious History. I smiled.

The seeds. I had so many seeds. When Clare had asked me to be keeper of the seeds, neither of us had known my mother and father's role in the Movement. Now that I knew how dangerous a cache of seeds was, I couldn't put Ma in jeopardy. Yet there were too many to carry with me. I considered throwing them in the garbage, or planting them, but that felt like a betrayal of trust. Then I thought of Arturo—his yard, the basement, the business he and his grandfather ran. I didn't want to explain. I rode over early in the morning and left a box with a note on his doorstep.

Then I did what Clare and Dante didn't have the luxury of doing. I left letters for Ana, Ma, and Rose so they wouldn't worry—or report me missing.

I needed to find answers, and aside from Ana, I no longer knew whom to trust. It was up to me, Lily Gardener, to push through the darkness like the plant inside a seed. It was time to make my way in the world.

It was time to meet my father.

End of Book Two

Coming Next in the
SEED SAVERS SERIES

In *Seed Savers: Heirloom*, travel with Lily as she searches for her father and find out what happened to Clare and Dante after they reached Canada. Read the excerpt from *Heirloom* now and then order your book today!

RUNNING TO

Lily—September

People have asked what made me do it. Why, at thirteen years old, I left the safety of my home and set out on my own. Was I afraid, some asked; did I run in fear, like my friends before me? No. That wasn't it. I never saw myself as running away from something. I was *running to* something.

That summer, the one when it all began, was when Lily Gardener finally knew her name.

The morning I left, a drizzling rain blanketed the town, forcing me to remember it that way—hazy, obscured—merging in my memory with what Arturo had said. That there was something "off," repressive, about our city—"like a cloud covering it."

I experienced no pangs of remorse as I deposited my goodbye letters for Ma, Rose, and Ana. And rather than feeling sorry about Arturo, I felt warm leaving the seeds in his care.

With one last look at my hometown, I boarded the bus, one of only three passengers departing that early September morning. I sat right up front, the mindset of looking forward. I would find James Gardener.

Mentally, I gathered up everything I knew about my father—so very little. I never knew him, and worse yet, he never knew me. By the time I was born, he was already in custody, soon to be locked up. I wondered if Ma had visited him during the sham trial or if he had ever held me. The pain of my mom's deception needled me like a sliver in my shoe. An anger I couldn't quite extinguish, yet barely acknowledged, simmered within me.

Looking back, I understand why my mom did what she did. But then, that day on the bus, I felt betrayed by the only parent I'd ever known. So I chose to look away from Ma. I convinced myself that I was my father's child. My father was a fighter, a leader, a writer. Someone who defied the status quo, risking everything. I would find him; we would fight together.

Ma had given me an allowance for as long as I could remember. I was never as grateful for this as I was now. Rarely having much to spend it on, I had saved quite a lot—the sum total currently bulging deep in my pocket, minus the chunk I'd used for a ticket to Florida. True, I didn't know if my dad really was in Cuba as Ana said he might be, but in case he was, I'd be that much closer. Besides, I'd always dreamed of going to Florida—who doesn't?

It would be a long trip giving me time to think about what to do next. I knew shuttles from Florida to Cuba left every hour but I wasn't sure how I would board. I considered stowing away but eventually decided my best option would be a fake letter of permission from my parents. I hoped by then to have made contact with "friends." I had a few stops planned farther north in Florida, intending to meet Seed Savers. Maybe they could confirm or pinpoint my father's whereabouts.

I reached into my pocket—not the one with the wad of cash, but another one—and pulled out the paper from Ana, the elderly mentor who had first taught my friends and me about seeds and gardening. I'd been surprised at the crowded list of names and numbers hand-printed neatly in tiny writing. I studied the paper, looking at the long list, trying to make sense of it. The names, for the most part, were listed alphabetically by last name. The numbers differed. Some were obvious street addresses or telecom numbers, but others . . . I wasn't sure—a code? The two letters ending each entry were obviously abbreviations for the fifty-one states.

Florida had seven listings. If only I could decipher the rest of the info and find someone like Ana who could tell me more, help me find my dad, provide a place to stay . . .

I pondered my last conversation with Ana. I had started blubbering about my dad. Revealed to her that I saw myself as being like him, shared how I too, loved to write. I'd complained about Ma and the way she disliked my writing.

"Lily, your mom is trying to protect you. She knows your dad's powerful words helped destroy your family. I'm sure she is proud of you and your writing. Please try to understand," Ana had said. And then she stunned me by telling me to do something contrary to my mom's wishes. "However, please don't stop writing. Writing is an act of reflecting. And the function of reflectors, after all, is to catch the light and shine it out. The Movement needs you, just like it needed your parents."

I liked that idea, that I was a reflector. That I could catch a ray of truth, like light, and shine it farther and wider.

Clare, my best friend, had tried unsuccessfully to journal—she had two abandoned diaries and a spiral notebook—and once, in exasperation, she had asked how I did it, this filling of notebooks, this incessant writing. I told her that if she had as many voices in her head as I did she wouldn't have to ask.

Clare had laughed hysterically. But the thing is, I was being perfectly honest. There's no easy way to describe how my brain often felt, feels. Cluttered. Like being in a room full of people, a room with bad acoustics, the cumulative noise of countless conversations roaring and crashing into a deafening din. Then slowly, as the room empties, the voices stop one by one, and at last there is this peaceful silence when everyone has gone.

That's how I write. It's *why* I write. To take the voices out of my head and confine them to bars on the paper. To have peace.

Grateful for a window seat, I stared out at the changing landscape. Thirteen, and I'd never travelled more than 96 kilometers from home. The urban sprawl through which the bus crawled was ugly and dilapidated. But the open land in between had its moments: gently rolling hills, golden plains with snakes of green along creeks and rivers, unidentifiable agribusiness crops.

There were no signs posted to identify the crops, reminding me how little I knew about the food I ate. Protein, Carbos, Vitees, Sweeties, and Snacks had always been enough. It was no longer enough. I wanted to know what was growing out there. I wanted to know what was in my food. I wanted to see what it looked like before it became the plastic-wrapped square or circle I called lunch.

Were those beans? I pressed my hands up against the bus window trying hard to make out the plants on the other side of the glass. I'd grown beans back in the vacant lot. I wanted to stop the bus and jump out. We were moving too fast for my inexperienced eyes to decipher.

Here and there abandoned homes presented more to ponder. The once quaint houses and old red barns were now forgotten and fading ghosts of history, falling in on themselves and grown over with weeds, shrubs, and flowers. Family farms from the past, I figured. The ancient barns were dwarfed by the shiny silver megastructures of today's corporate/government-controlled farms. I closed my eyes and imagined how it had been before. I thought about what Ana had told me, that GRIM was losing its stranglehold, that Seed Savers were gathering strength. I remembered Arturo's comments about California. A hope for the future surged within me.

When I opened my eyes, I was startled by the sea of gigantic three-pronged towers, arms spinning. These must be the wind turbine farms I'd read about and seen pictures of on educational Monitor shows. I wondered what they sounded like. My soul was torn between the grand idea that I would make a difference in this world and the countering thought of how small and insignificant I was in a place filled with such enormous structures.

On and on we rolled, past more abandonment and desolation. Areas where not only the buildings were discarded and hopeless, but the land itself. Places too expensive to water and where adequate rain no longer fell. Land parched and treated so poorly that it had lost its ability to be productive and was tossed aside like so much trash.

Even the birds flew over without stopping.

From my cool seat on the bus I watched the ripply waves rising off the pavement, a testament to the devil-hot heat out there. I closed my eyes against the depressing sea of emptiness, clicked on my music, and willed myself to fade away for just a little while.

DON'T MISS THESE BOOKS IN THE SEED SAVERS SERIES

TREASURE
(Seed Savers 1)

LILY
(Seed Savers 2)

Releasing soon from Flying Books House

HEIRLOOM
(Seed Savers 3)

KEEPER
(Seed Savers 4)

UNBROKEN
(Seed Savers 5)

FLYING BOOKS HOUSE

FlyingBooksHouse.com

SPECIAL NOTE FROM THE AUTHOR

I have been poking seeds into the ground ever since I can remember. I grew up on a farm—berries mostly—and my mom planted a huge garden each year. My job as a child was to place seeds in the furrows Mom dug. I still eat mostly according to the seasons, including harvesting and preserving about 100 pounds of peaches each summer.

The historical political references in *Seed Savers* series are factual although I've changed the names of the corporations.

I have met farmers who were visited by "the seed police" —men watching them on their farms and bringing lawsuits meant to shut them down after the farmer's crops were con-taminated by the GM seeds of their neighbors.

On another note, I've seen children pull up veggies ran-domly in a garden in search of carrots because they didn't know what carrot tops looked like.

And, of course, there is an organization called *Seed Savers Exchange* with whom I am not affiliated in any way.

What Lily does, the planting of vegetables in vacant lots or waysides, is known as guerrilla gardening. Check the Resources section to find out more.

There are many wonderful gardeners and seed savers in the world today. Maybe you are one of them. If you're not, you can be!

Sandra Smith

RESOURCES TO CONTINUE
THE CONVERSATION

GM Food Awareness
http://www.kidsrighttoknow.com/

Saving Seeds
https://www.seedsavers.org/

Gardening Programs for Kids: American Horticultural Society & Junior Master Gardeners
http://ahsgardening.org/gardening-programs/youth-gardening/ncygs
http://jmgkids.us/

More Food and Food Politics
http://michaelpollan.com/
https://www.foodpolitics.com/about/
http://vandanashiva.com/

Guerrilla Gardening
https://en.wikipedia.org/wiki/Guerrilla_gardening
http://www.latimes.com/food/dailydish/la-fo-ron-finley-project-
20170503-story.html

Make Fresh Peppermint & Chamomile Tea
https://www.thespruceeats.com/easy-fresh-mint-tea-recipe-766391
https://simpleseasonal.com/how-to/how-to-make-chamomile-tea-
with-fresh-flowers

Sources in Researching *Lily*
https://www.thesimpledollar.com/does-a-basement-greenhouse-
really-save-money/
https://www.gardeningchannel.com/grow-vegetables-indoors/

ACKNOWLEDGMENTS

Thanks to all the people who continue to encourage and support me in this crazy endeavor of being an author. To the early readers and helpers of the series: Aileen, Tracy, Anita, Rita, and more.

Also a big thank you to my new team at Flying Books House: Shannon, Sharon, and Alan.

As always, thank you to my husband and kids. I love you guys.

ABOUT THE AUTHOR

Sandra Smith grew up on a farm with a tremendously large garden. She maintains that if you can't taste the soil on a carrot, it's not fresh enough.

Today, Sandra lives in the city with her husband, cats, and backyard hens. She grows a small urban garden every summer. When she's not gardening or turning tomatoes into spaghetti sauce, Sandra often writes poetry or novels inspired by her garden. She is the author of the popular series, *Seed Savers*.

Sandra enjoys visiting schools and gardening events to talk about *Seed Savers* and food in general. Find out more by visiting SeedSaversSeries.com or look for her on Twitter at @AuthorSSmith.

SeedSaversSeries.com